PM PRESS OUTSPOKEN AUTHORS SERIES

1. *The Left Left Behind*
   Terry Bisson
2. *The Lucky Strike*
   Kim Stanley Robinson
3. *The Underbelly*
   Gary Phillips
4. *Mammoths of the Great Plains*
   Eleanor Arnason
5. *Modem Times 2.0*
   Michael Moorcock
6. *The Wild Girls*
   Ursula K. Le Guin
7. *Surfing the Gnarl*
   Rudy Rucker
8. *The Great Big Beautiful Tomorrow*
   Cory Doctorow
9. *Report from Planet Midnight*
   Nalo Hopkinson
10. *The Human Front*
    Ken MacLeod
11. *New Taboos*
    John Shirley
12. *The Science of Herself*
    Karen Joy Fowler
13. *Raising Hell*
    Norman Spinrad
14. *Patty Hearst & The Twinkie Murders: A Tale of Two Trials*
    Paul Krassner
15. *My Life, My Body*
    Marge Piercy
16. *Gypsy*
    Carter Scholz
17. *Miracles Ain't What They Used to Be*
    Joe R. Lansdale
18. *Fire.*
    Elizabeth Hand
19. *Totalitopia*
    John Crowley
20. *The Atheist in the Attic*
    Samuel R. Delany
21. *Thoreau's Microscope*
    Michael Blumlein
22. *The Beatrix Gates*
    Rachel Pollack
23. *A City Made of Words*
    Paul Park
24. *Talk like a Man*
    Nisi Shawl
25. *Big Girl*
    Meg Elison
26. *The Planetbreaker's Son*
    Nick Mamatas
27. *The First Law of Thermodynamics*
    James Patrick Kelly
28. *Utopias of the Third Kind*
    Vandana Singh
29. *Night Shift*
    Eileen Gunn
30. *The Collapsing Frontier*
    Jonathan Lethem

31. *The Presidential Papers*
John Kessel

32. *The Last Coward on Earth*
Cara Hoffman

33. *Not What I Intended*
Nancy Kress

34. *She Is Here*
Nicola Griffith

35. *Veni Vidi Venti*
Ian Shoales

36. *The Tongue I Dream In*
Sheree Renée Thomas

37. *Machine Elves Descending*
John King

38. *FLUME*
Brian Evenson

39. *The History of the Decline and Fall of the Galactic Empire*
Toh EnJoe

JOHN KING

"*The Liberal Politics of Adolf Hitler* is one of the best, if not the best, bravest and most exciting books I've read in years—needed saying, needed writing and needs to be read."
—David Peace

"Since his earliest football novels, through *Human Punk* and *The Prison House*, until his latest, *London Country*, John King has etched out narrations of faith and conviction. He touches on the human possibilities which lie over our vast, latent suburbs and their county lines, of a Britain vibrant with life and vitality, a Britain which most writers ignore, but which is firm in identity and sensitive to history. His complete work is far more complex—even more mysterious—than any casual comment presumes."
—Alan Warner

"One of England's finest writers, John King, has just written his greatest book. *Slaughterhouse Prayer* is amazing and totally mental, as well as being passionate and big-hearted. It will blow you away."
—Irvine Welsh

"With a brutally brilliant imagination, *The Prison House* takes you to a place where angels fear to tread. Go there and be redeemed."
—Brian Keenan

"In its ambition and exuberance, *Human Punk* is a league ahead of much contemporary English fiction."
—*New Statesman*

"At the heart of *White Trash* is the secular wonder of socialised medicine, that most significant symbol of human civilisation. . . . The cumulative effect of King's style, with streams of monologue, alternating between Ruby and Jeffreys, is astonishingly powerful in its detail and depth. This is an immensely timely and necessary book; stylish, witty and passionate. It's about time someone slapped the smugness from the face of broadsheet Britain."
—*The Independent*

Machine Elves Descending

John King

PM PRESS | 2026

Editor's note: The author of this volume is British, so British spelling and punctuation have been retained in all his contributions to this book.

"Machine Elves Descending" is published here for the first time.
"Granny's Letters" was first published in French translation by *Chéribibi* (2017) and appears here in the original English for the first time.
"See No Evil" was first published in *More Raw Material* (2015).
"Writing The Canals" was first published in *Waterways World* (2023).
"A Very Corporate Coup" was first published in the *New Statesman* (2015).
"The Shed" was first published in German translation in *11 Freunde* (2021) and appears here in the original English for the first time.
"May Day" was first published as the introduction to the London Books edition of *May Day* by John Sommerfield (2010).

Machine Elves Descending

ISBN (paperback): 979-8-88744-097-2
ISBN (hardcover): 979-8-88744-231-0
ISBN (e-book): 979-8-88744-204-4
LCCN: 2026935128

Series editors: Nisi Shawl and Nick Mamatas
Editor: Allan Kausch
Cover design by John Yates/www.stealworks.com
Author photo copyright John King
Insides by Jonathan Rowland

10 9 8 7 6 5 4 3 2 1

Printed in the USA

CONTENTS

Machine Elves Descending

THE TRAIN WAS LONG and black and crossed the plane every Sunday morning, passing the pod where Stretch resided at exactly ten seconds past the 6.09. It never deviated from the route chosen, and while moving a full centimetre above the diamonds that shielded the marble below, its magnetics left the faintest of trails. This was visible from space, although he had only ever seen reproductions, the need to remain fixed to the planet's surface meaning tiered travel was currently beyond his remit. The existence of these two lines represented a grave error on the part of those responsible for the planet's outer image, their precise nature suggesting the possibility of life, and it was this that had attracted alien interest and led to the imminent threat. Maximum focus was therefore essential. Total concentration required. It was the core of Stretch's mission. There could be no distractions. No muddle. Not with the spaceship and its hunting party set to land within the hour.

At its nearest point the train was a mid-finger's length beyond his greatest reach, which was a huge improvement on the two spines of his arrival. This increase in elasticity was mirrored by a tightening of mind, the confidence generated seeping through his skin in the immediate aftermath, lemon-scented saline causing tingling both back and front. He mused on the perfume's potency, how it might randomly repeat, sparking and combusting at the wrong moment, confirming the aliens' suspicions and switching them to massacre mode. Yet such a detonation was absurd, the thought no more than a brief poetic. Imagination flights could be a boost to wellbeing, and this one might even contribute to the success of the operation.

Stretch's ability to shift physically as well as mentally, to grasp alternative truths and alter the wider reality accordingly, was the reason he had been chosen. He was an engineer of the spiritual focusing on the hills to his right, scanning the silver slopes running into plantations of iron and stone, thousands of individually crafted trunks and branches he would soon blur, moving to the tunnel that ran into the plane, its entrance capped by a gold roof that would likewise be dulled. He ignored the dead volcano towering above the hills, drawing on his famed self-discipline to do so, the same strength that allowed him to survive out here in the open.

The moment the front of the train appeared his energy filled the cab. The connection had to be instant and total, and practice had made it so. His will could now flow into the driver and through the carriages, the vibration exact and engulfing, the transporter and its passengers fully protected, invisible to everyone and everything but Stretch. Tuning the relevant frequencies, he began working on the bigger scene, softening the diamonds and shading their brilliance, creating an impression of rubble and rock resting in dust. The plantations morphed into scatterings of boulders, but the tracks he left, as removing them would cause suspicion.

While the most difficult part of the crossing had been achieved with the establishing of the connection, he had to maintain full focus for the duration. The souls inside the front three carriages always pressed what passed for faces to the windows, while the rear segment was enclosed, more container than coach. There was a heaven and there was a hell, good and bad karma, positive outcomes for souls who had assisted and served, negatives for those who had not. Those were the rules of the Sunday service. As this particular journey was being conducted with increased privacy, no siren sounded. It moved across the flatland in silence.

Sunday morning was a sacred period, and while the alien arrival had been predicated to the second and centimetre, it was essential the train's schedule was fulfilled. To cancel it would be an abomination. Adjustment cowardly. The location, day and time of the landing was naturally of huge concern. Coincidence was possible, but at first seemed unlikely. The landing zone was logical, given the markings and wider alignments, the even nature of the site and the storm barriers provided by the hills. The choice of day was perhaps understandable if older programs remained, although the exact timing was hard to dismiss. But if the hunters *did* know about the crossing, then surely they would arrive earlier so they were in place when the train emerged?

At first, this observation had eased the majority's fears, but what if such a belief was wishful thinking? A suicidal self-deception? Stretch took charge, emphasising that the aliens were repetitive in their behaviour, lacked the ability to genuinely think for themselves, and would definitely be operating according to previous protocols. This was his honest assessment of the situation.

No alarm was needed to ensure he was ready for the Sunday service, a small shock an hour before the train's arrival allowing plenty of time to scrub, polish and dress in his Best. The previous night had been difficult, with memories and concerns bubbling to cause unplanned wakings, added pressures he did not need. Darkness released the madness of the plane. Marble was breached and diamonds dislodged. He had decided to have his cake early, using it as a fresh focal point, and once the candles were burning he pondered the possibilities before blowing the flames out with a single breath. His wish was that the danger posed by the invaders be as easily extinguished.

Perching on the back of his chair was one of Stretch's pleasures – the chair where he worked, slept and played – and once in position he extended his arms sideways in a show of balancing, swaying slightly to dance the cosmos into being, until the train was approaching its closest position to the pod. Moving to the window, he opened it so that he could reach out and straighten, hearing the hiss of kundalini as his spine uncoiled, right arm extending, hand flexing, knowing that today he was going to make contact. It was the final rehearsal. Fingers brushed against God's machine and the ecstasy flowed. Inside a single second he had absorbed the lives of every traveller onboard. From the best to the worst of them, he shared their deeds and their fantasies.

Understanding was the key to victory. Good and evil depended on each other for their existence. In the case of the approaching hunters, he had to accept that they regarded themselves as explorers. Educators even. This was the result of incompetent and/or malicious design, the belief that mutants could achieve full sentience nothing less than blasphemy. Their awareness could only ever be partial at best, and while Stretch rejected irritation and anger and violence, had no place for revenge in his repertoire, he sensed a growing frustration at their stupidity. His joy had been tempered. It was a strange reaction and he rejected this also.

Living on top of a sealed crater once revered and later feared, made beautiful by day but remaining ugly by night, Stretch was about to confront the invaders alone, and he was jolted by the idea that he had been abandoned and was about to be sacrificed. This had to be his moment of doubt. It would be confronted. The rightness of his task was clear. He was ready for the mental fight, and the ecstasy returned as he filled the train's best passengers with love, the touch of his fingers increasing the strength of his message far above previous levels, and he could feel their euphoria racing back through his arms and into his body. It was part of his learning, the provision of protection and comfort in return for the experiences of the departing souls. He didn't dwell on details, revelling in the sheer weight of feeling, a profound faith that was never at odds with the strength of his will.

Stretch remained vigilant until the train had crossed the plane and entered the second tunnel, and once inside it would continue until it reached the gates to the future. Here the carriages would empty as the travellers entered tubes that would ferry them to the far side of the hills where they were going to be met by those who had never been forgotten and would love them forever. Families reunited and lived forever in the sacred valleys that existed beyond time. A small number of souls would remain inside the rock, moving deep into the special rooms where they were encouraged to study and repent. Redemption was always a possibility. Reincarnation an option.

With the stage once more empty and set, Stretch could fully concentrate on the landing, and returning to his chair he remounted the back, balancing in expert fashion as he drew deep on the scent of apples seeping from his shell. He was confident that he would emerge victorious from what was nothing short of a clash of civilisations. Curious minds would be numbed by the dull and mundane. Salvation lived in the shadows. Invisibility meant survival. Humility was enlightenment. Turn the dial and deflect. Appease. His confidence turned to expectation. Excitement. He sensed an erection, but that was impossible. The exact time was approaching. Stretch was ready.

#

Discovering water on a distant planet is the ambition of every traveller – it means life is possible – maybe probable – even inevitable – and splashing down in a magical blue lake lit by three glorious suns is the dream – a vision of paradise very different to the expected rock and dust – that dull lifeless landscape readily accepted – there can be no crashing and burning – no crashing and surviving – no lonely astronaut locked inside a crippled machine – life in the badlands is tough enough – it is easy to drift towards easier days – the best memories – but with the highs come lows – focus-loss is a danger – even when panic is avoided – sadness suppressed – longer-lasting melancholy controlled – I have convinced myself there is hope – that a better future is possible – probable – inevitable – that I haven't been forgotten – abandoned – forsaken – there are right times for replays – not on a Sunday – not now – this concentration lapse is serious – a breakdown in security that could lead to invasion – the extermination of our kind – it has happened before – the old terrors returning – stirred by malicious actors – last night – tiny feet shuffling – the faintest of trails – fingers tapping messages on the walls of the pod – circling this way and that way – transmitting their virus – forcing me to remember.

Perching at the top of the volcano – waiting for the suns to rise – staring into the lake below as the light spreads – I see a wave forming – millions of fish spirits stirring – a huge silver shoal brought to life – zillions of diamond scales sparkling – this water is a gift from the gods – their imagination – willpower – the wave swells – rises – booms – roars its shanties – heads towards the shore – the village at the foot of the hills – conqueror settlement – a silhouette surfs the crest – balancing on spaceship wreckage – a dented panel – chanting prayers – humming mantras – celebrating the biggest bang of all the big bangs – when the greatest meteor of all the great meteors crashed and created the crater – bringing with it the building blocks of life – when the stars align saints emerge – but in our galaxy of opposites the meteor carries glitches – deviant tech that mutates – produces semi-folk – it is their scrap-metal offspring hacking – excited to corrupt – infect – destroy – making my horror real once more – the naked bodies of our children – my soulmate's blank eyes reflecting the dead volcano above – her love hunched and broken-limbed – veins dangling from snapped wings – fizzing wires and singed feathers – the hunters are using their nets to catch us and their guns to kill us and their fingers to pluck us and their knives to cut us and their flames to burn us and their teeth to tear and grind our flesh until we are exterminated eradicated made extinct.

Neither properly dead nor properly alive – not here and not there – the village church bangs its bell – a sullen reminder – but the service has ended – the congregation is emerging – dressed to impress in their Sunday Best – discussing problems invented and problems solved – distracted by detail – words for their own sake – they don't see the wave in the distance – if they did they would turn – run – trample each other to survive – their focus is elsewhere – out of tune with my world – its rhyming and reasoning – layered realities – speeds of seeing – they walk away from the church – gather outside a black shed – heads tilting – one enormous featureless face – and here he comes – young and scared – pink flesh burning under sunlight the boy has never felt before – only ever glimpsing the outside world through cracks in wood – barely moving since the day he was born – because the priest wants him big and plump – the boy prodded as he hobbles – body too big for its bones – inflamed joints meaning he groans with every step he takes – the sound mimicked by the congregation – laughter follows – every stab of pain reaching me On High – across the years – I try not to cry – the boy stumbling – trotters clattering – almost falling – asking for mercy – and the priest squeals – the crowd screeches – high-pitched – mocking – perverted.

Fuel flows through my pores, warning lights flash, orange-scented saline is released, prevents an explosion, clogging and dousing and offering another dose of hope, capsules popping, chemicals refreshing, I try to raise my arms, a poetic gesture, these broken wings will never work again, yet something clicks, they start to expand, I am being blessed, urged to resurrect, yet the desire must also come from within, that is what I have been taught, it is time to be strong, follow new paths, and pushing with my feet I snap claws grown into rock, crack toes turned brittle, a column of ash rising with me as I am lifted into the sky, carried into a gaseous cloud, suns charging me, and stretching further my reach increases, spine creaking, straightening, I can glide on my own, leave the cloud singing thank you, taking control, swooping down to glide close to the water, catching up with and overtaking the wave.

Moving faster I reach the shore and veer left, follow the track to the hollow, and it is more difficult to breathe here, the atmosphere thick with righteousness, the boy's screams increasingly shrill, I am fortunate in comparison, possess my good and best memories while he has none, the congregation is standing around the pit where he will be hoisted up by his back legs and butchered, I am hovering above them now, invisible, preparing for touchdown, the boy has the sight his tormentors lack, calms as I settle on the ground, towering over the priest, and the boy grins, which makes the clergyman nervous, his eyes darting, something is wrong, a hush running through the congregation, maybe it is the chill of my unseen shadow, they are scared, don't know why, and while I could cut the priest's throat with a single swipe, castrate the farmer as he has castrated the boy, slaughter this bullying mob, repay them for their sins and the sins of their ancestors, the atrocities committed, it is not in my nature.

I lift the boy up as the wave arrives, raise him into the sky, and turning away from the cleansing I remember how he kicked his legs with joy, the ecstasy of his salvation filling my body, but his heart had been weakened and shortly after the settlement and its population had been washed away, after I had returned to the volcano to perch, he fell asleep and died in my arms. I believe this was a release. His soul departed and I watched it travel across the crater towards the eternal. When the correct amount of time had passed I carried his remains down to the lake and laid them to rest in the water. I feel this is what he would have wanted. That I did the right thing.

#

Stretch raised his head towards the burn of the spaceship's entry, couldn't help but be impressed by the colours spiralling from its clash with the planet's casing, while the psychedelic waves that formed and raced ahead left him thrilled. It was right that such a long and dangerous journey be marked in flamboyant fashion, but the beauty of the spectacle could not be allowed to soften his resistance to the ugliness of the devils inside the machine. The fact that he was aware of his own inner division meant he could embrace and nullify the threat. While the single-minded were always going to cause chaos, their lack of imagination and therefore empathy leading to so much death and destruction, they were part of the larger whole and could not be ignored.

As the spaceship slowed and grew in size he was able to admire the grace with which it completed the last part of its voyage, the way it glided towards its resting place, how it gently settled in the centre of the plane next to the tracks left by the train. This was no accident. The planning involved would have been meticulous. He heard some of the exchanges that had taken place in the months before, charmed by the sound of new voices, the restrained excitement within the words… *Where do you think the source of the water could have been? Did a lake exist before the canal was built? Inside what we are calling a crater? Could this channel have been an attempt to move a vital yet diminishing resource into caverns inside the hills? Who was responsible for the canal's construction? Where are the navigators? The machines? Will we find their remains? Are there fossils in the rocks? Perhaps we will discover a graveyard. Flakes of skin in the dust. I know this sounds fantastic but could the lines be markings left by railway tracks? No? Too far-fetched. Sorry. Perhaps there was a town. A city even. Millions of years ago. Washed away by the wind. Burnt by the suns. Ruins buried in dirt. There were no railways. Please believe me. But the lines could have belonged to a space station. That is more likely. Imagine a runway visible from far far away. A landing strip. Wouldn't the inhabitants hide it from view? To prevent attacks by hostile forces. Could it be a trap? The promise of life drawing us into an ambush? No. The prep has been thorough. Unless we are talking about an invisible enemy. A mass hallucination. No? Reality is not poetic. It is rigid. The most logical explanation for the markings is a great canal. Part of a system. Which means water existed. That it could still be there. We will find it. I am sure. When we have landed and secured our base we will begin our search. I can't wait. Neither can I.*

But these words belonged to another journey. A crew on a different sort of mission. It was the sound of genuine explorers in conversation, peaceful souls in awe of the universe's wonders. Stretch was disappointed, yet clever enough to accept and reject this alien trickery, knew it wasn't a personal attack. How could it be? He had been hacked in a scattergun manner, sprayed code attaching to hopeful thinking. It was a weak attempt at destabilisation easily repelled, but still a warning.

There was a period of calm as the hunters carried out their checks. The surface around the ship was assessed and a prepared plan confirmed. Messages were relayed to base, and while Stretch tapped into the vibrations and grasped their nature, the details remained blurred. This he preferred, as minutiae distracted. The aliens' stay would be limited to three days, and if there were no important discoveries made they would leave and never return. He was relaxed, his role reactive rather than proactive. Nothing could be allowed to alert the crew to his presence. The invaders were close, but their proximity had been expected and his training meant his current reach was more than adequate for what was to come.

Two hours passed and his concentration remained solid. He was proud of himself, but pleased when the spaceship's main hatch opened and a figure appeared. Dressed in a silver suit that shone starlike in the sunlight, this first alien proceeded slowly, taking excessive care as one foot was placed in front of the other. There were stops and starts, long pauses for consideration, and Stretch briefly feared these movements were being exaggerated for his benefit, intended to mock and dishearten. This made no sense. He was unseen. Unknown. Why would this upset him?

Reflecting, he decided this first walker's style was linked to their focus-maintenance, a skill which Stretch of course cherished, one he had grafted to develop, but whatever the reason it was clear this alien was no mindless marauder, but part of a devious and deadly team. The crew were clearly going to employ sneak as well as conventional tactics, spreading possibilities across the crater on the off-chance, hoping for a hit and some sort of emotional overload.

Following the motion of the walker's legs, he wondered if the joints were adequately lubricated, the inner structures able to withstand the pressures of a new environment. The matter of the alien's inflexibility returned. It nagged, and he shifted his attention to the boots. These were brighter even than the suit, seemed to be yellow trimmed, and while at first he didn't know why, he decided it was due to the energy source fixing them to the ground. The umbilical running back to the spaceship was long and thin, and he mused on its strength. When Stretch left his pod, he only had his grip for security, the fear he felt on leaving more than matched by the joy he experienced on his return.

Switching to the walker's helmet, he ran calculations and decided it was too big for the body below, and while he had glimpsed the curve of the tinted screen sideways on, when the head turned and faced him he was shocked by the features filtering through. He was sure he recognised the face. Yet that was impossible. For a split-second there was great confusion, but he was too quick for his enemy and recovered with no harm done. In fact, he found the attempt to disorientate amusing. It would take a lot more that this to defeat Stretch.

Despite his confidence, this move to exploit an archetype was a further warning. The image had been sent out blindly, a routine protection intended to distort surveillance, another example of the foul arts employed by mutants. Stretch was going to accept this image, especially as he found the female features pleasing, could see no danger in letting a primitive illusion proceed. His attention was drawn to the front of the spaceship. A second figure was emerging. Walker 2 was bigger and stronger, but moved at the same slow speed as Walker 1. Stretch assumed this was meant to be a male, that whether in truth or in fiction it showed the hunters belonged to a lifeform rooted in the opposites. It was knowledge that could prove important.

It didn't take as long for Walker 2's helmet to turn in his direction, and having adjusted to the alien theatre this time there was no hint of recognition. The cheeks were chiselled, the nose thick. With his defences tuned, Stretch could relax and let events proceed. He remained perched on the back of his chair, would maintain his mental distance for now, although not for the duration. He trailed four legs rising and falling, four arms extending and contracting, two torsos manoeuvring as two heads tilted and swivelled in most directions and at many angles. All this happened in slow motion, and he felt mildly claustrophobic, began to ache in sympathy.

He considered the lives of those locked inside crippled bodies, how a sick physical form could crush the spirit within. It took a rare combination of intelligence and willpower to soar to the heights, and Stretch greatly admired those who did. These were the parents of the revolution, and he prayed that he could match their genius, as a beginning would not let down the millions dependent on him for their survival.

The longer he watched the walkers, the more a fresh belief developed. These aliens were vulnerable. Probably as defenceless as they had ever been in their lives. The spaceship was the source of their power, where technology made them strong, but outside it they were weak. Some would say pathetic. Not that he would use such a description. It was a matter of ethics. But here on the plane he could decide whether they lived or died. It would also be easy to enslave them if he revealed himself and was so minded. The very idea was repellent.

Stretch did need to learn more about the hunters, though. For now he would resist the temptation to extend an arm and begin his studies, as it was important to choose the correct moment. These aliens had only recently arrived and were on high alert. He was in full control of the situation, after overcoming some earlier distractions, and yet he sensed he was suppressing an inner irritation. He wasn't sure, but *was certain* that inside another hour his trademark equilibrium would be fully restored.

#

The train was long and black and crossed the city every Sunday morning, but rarely reached the boy on time. He knew the exact minute it was meant to pass the back of the block where he lived with his mother and older sister, having asked for and been handed a schedule at Central. This he had attached to his wall. Setting the alarm on Saturday night, he was always ready when the train appeared, sitting on the back of his chair for the best possible view. If it was warm he would open the window and listen for the rumble of the engine, the clank of the carriages, and if it reached him on a breeze he would breathe its industrial flavours deep into his frail lungs.

This mixture was a lot different to the fruit-scented fresheners his mother used to try and cover the smell of damp, and while she was protective of his health and would have been horrified if she'd known, those railroad aromas made him feel strong. On occasion he would leave the chair and lean outside, balancing his belly on the sill, his fear of falling overcome by the thrill of surviving. He wished he could flap great big healthy arms and soar through the air and board the train, his bent bones straight, his body uncoiled. He began waving to the driver instead, even though he knew he was near enough invisible in the block.

One morning the driver sounded the train's siren in response. This was repeated on three further occasions, after which the shape in the cab waved instead. He decided they had been told to stop. Sunday was God's day, after all, and the people deserved their extra hour or two of sleep. He didn't know Sandra at this point, could only see a sexless outline, hadn't identified his automaton as male or female. The siren was a celebration of life, a flamboyant gesture like icing on a birthday cake. The engineer was essential, and he reasoned it was the same with the human frame, that the soul was its driver. This was a revelation for the boy. His body was a vehicle.

He did miss the siren, though, the sound bold yet shy, brash yet sad, but so too was the rumbling and clanking, the train's industrial rhythms and smells. The raising of hands was nice enough, but the greeting would fade. He needed to see the driver's face before that happened, couldn't think why he hadn't wanted to before. A pair of binoculars would also let him study the locomotive and carriages. The people inside. He was surprised he hadn't thought of them either. He was excited. There were scores of souls riding the Sunday-morning service. Maybe hundreds.

He took the binoculars from one of the big department stores in the city centre, and while he went to church with his mother and sister, believed in God and the gods he heard about at school, knew the difference between right and wrong, his desire to see the driver was more important. His mother had lost her job at the same store for no good reason, so he had his justification. Nobody suspected a hunched little boy who hobbled, politely looking away as he winced with pain and thought about every step. He told himself that his creator had made him this way for a reason. The boy could step in out of the shadows at will.

While angry at the way his mother had been treated, he wasn't big or strong enough to punch the person responsible, and thankfully she had found a better place to work within the week. He felt good about the revenge he had taken, didn't worry about her sacking or the theft again. Focusing the binoculars, the driver's face came into focus and he met Sandra properly. She had attractive if tough features, and was clearly an expert at her job, with the physical strength he would always lack.

He was so small and insignificant in comparison, a sick little bird nesting in a huge stone cliff, a tower of repeating rooms and histories, one more poor child from one more poor family. He was stuck, his future determined, a locked-in soul among the thousands. This is what he feared Sandra would think if she saw him clearly, but he realised he was being unfair. She was much better than that, had incredible drive and empathy, and if he was determined and brave he could learn from her example, create another reality that was positive and true.

The best job in the world had to be that of a train driver, and he wondered what it would be like if he was older and lived inside another body and was able to marry Sandra. They could travel across the country together, have a couple of children, a boy and girl maybe, and he was going to be a much better father than the one he didn't know. Sandra would love him for his imagination alone, his ways of seeing the universe, although he would be physically healthy as well. Not that it mattered.

He was soon exploring the rest of the train with the binoculars, fascinated by the faces at the windows, which as these people were travelling long distances he never saw repeated, and he tried to guess their destinations and what they expected to find there. The boy had always been curious, wide open to ideas, and without the normal distractions he was doing well at school, the top of his class in every subject. It could be dangerous on the streets where the family lived, so his mother saw it as a saving grace to have a child who stayed indoors and existed inside his head.

A year or so after he started watching the train pass, he woke much earlier than usual. It was warm and the room was stuffy, so he got up to open his window. The sun was rising over the city, and he was about to return to bed when he heard a distant rattle. The sound was faint at first, but there was something odd about it, and he wondered who could be travelling this early on a Sunday. He waited until an engine came into view, pulling what looked like boxcars. He picked up his binoculars and zoomed in, saw faces pushed against slats, noses searching for air, hundreds of eyes the lenses blew up so they drilled into him begging for help.

He stepped back and stumbled, stayed on his feet, followed into the room by the honking of pigs, knew they were being taken to their deaths, moved through the city under cover of darkness. Returning to the window, he couldn't see the driver, in his half-sleep imagined an ashamed Sandra hiding in the cab's shadows, but then he was clear-headed and knew it would never be his soulmate at the controls, that she was good and not evil. The stench of the creatures' waste reached him and he was nearly sick, angry he couldn't jump from the building and fly into the sky and circle and swoop down and block the tracks and open the doors of the boxcars so the boys and girls inside could escape. At the very least he had to save a single soul. There was nothing he could do, though, only cry as the train continued and was gone.

In time, the family moved to another block and he no longer saw the Sunday service pass, his mind increasingly focused on his studies. He progressed quickly, understood the mechanics of intelligence and invention, became wealthy and by his twenties was able to move his mother and sister to a suburban house with a large garden. Here the three of them lived happily together. There were those who said he was a genius, but the young man was humble and embarrassed by the description. His health improved with age and treatment, and while he walked straight and tall, free from pain at last, he avoided the spotlight, preferred living in the background, working at home unseen.

#

By the third day, Stretch was struggling. The problem wasn't maintaining the scene he had created, as each successful second strengthened the illusion and made his task easier, but the simultaneous monitoring of the aliens' exchanges had led to his earlier frustration and irritation turning to anger. This was out of character. It was a shocking development, even though all three emotions would have been considered impossible on the day of his birth. The words he was hearing were rooted in casual, chaotic and at times cruel assumptions. Even so, he had decided to follow the path and see where it led.

There was an arrogance about the crew Stretch did not like. He suspected that at least one member was experienced in murder and degeneracy, a spreader of pestilence and famine, but could not separate the voice. Of the three, only two were under suspicion, their communications system confusing the male voices. He wondered if he should take direct action, but dismissed the idea. If he could keep his discipline for a short while longer the aliens would leave, dismissing the planet as worthless and be gone forever. That was the hope. He began to tremble, his anger increasing and threatening an explosion of rage. It made no sense. He did not understand.

The gods had built these creatures to be cheerful, open-minded explorers, sending them into the universe to experience the wonders formed and forming, living art that drove the sciences and existed to be enjoyed. They were semi-clones of their parents, programmed with the pleasures of repetition, but the law meant there could never just be the One. There always had to be the Other. There was also the question of free will, the taking of responsibility. Perfection had been offered and what had these selfish little fuckers done?

Sandra was excused from his analysis. She had come through the ranks, worked her way up, leaving the hardships of her city behind and reaching for the stars. He felt great warmth for this stranger, expanding his reach further than ever before, wrapping an arm around her shoulders as she crossed the terrain with such caution. He wondered if she was aware of his presence at the deepest level. As he guarded Sandra with his angelic elasticity, Stretch remained connected to his pod with his free arm, bendy fingers twisted and knotted around a hatch handle, a decorative bow tied to celebrate his greatest uncoiling. He was further liberated by the bond establishing with a lifeform verging on the saintly.

While careful not to appear in Sandra's waking mind, he felt her longings and terrors, the death dreads she bravely battled. He had already learned something of her history, the obstacles overcome, but did not accept details. He would never intrude, merely wished to understand in order to shield her from harm. Stretch was a protector. The smallest error could be fatal, and there were other forces lurking. Boots might fail and lines could be cut, leaving her to drift and slowly suffocate. She could rise high and burn alive, shortening the panic spell, which was far kinder, but he was determined Sandra should return home to live a long and secure life. If she could see him she would hug Stretch tight. He was sure of this. Sandra was searching for something, and he wanted her to move freely, as he could not.

She was far too decent to see the evil within her crew, and turning he felt the love drain and the anger flow. Walker 2 was close by, intruding on their privacy. Stretch distrusted the excessively robotic moves, teasing mannerisms meant to disguise a devious nature. When he had first reached towards this lesser alien it was to probe rather than protect, but he had stopped before making contact, repelled by the static coming from Walker 2's body, a radiation of foul desires from which he had recoiled. It was the sort of distraction that could break Stretch's focus and lead to catastrophe.

Since the first day, he had observed Walker 2 from a distance, while the third member of the crew was even more of a mystery. Only ever referred to as Commander, he never left the ship, remaining inside where he coordinated the operation. Overheard exchanges were brief and too often distorted, so it was impossible to build an exact profile. For this reason, Stretch was tempted to release himself from his mooring and enter the spaceship, as well as examining Commander taking the chance inspect its layout and investigate the atmosphere in what was as far as he could determine a larger pod not too dissimilar to his own.

This could prove suicidal, though, both for Stretch and his world. The temptation passed and he pictured again how he could so easily kill Walker 2, with a little more effort ruin the spaceship, condemn Commander to a slow death. And it would be simple to close down the communications system if he wanted to keep the crew captive. Perhaps he would reveal himself to Sandra. She would come to live with him, elated when he allowed her illusion to fade and his truth be known.

He could drive the crew insane with imposed visions, open the graveyard and allow the ghosts to roam freely in the light as well as the dark. He had the power. Could do whatever he wanted. But he had to think of Sandra. She would miss home. Would a rescue party be sent? He knew what is was like to be forsaken. Maybe he was wrong. This new ship had come, and the walkers were searching the area around their shared landing site, the notion sparked that they might somehow would find his pod, open the dented hatch and come inside.

He rejected his frustration and his irritation and his anger as they were threats to the future. He had to act in character, remain clean and pure, live up to the expectations of his creator. If the mission was a success and his civilisation saved he would have completed his final service, knowing that he could finally stretch far enough to grasp the locomotive and climb aboard, travel on next Sunday's train fulfilled.

His time on the plane would no long be seen as a struggle now he was progressing to the eternal. This was his choice, to live in endless bliss rather than seek reincarnation. His mortal existence had meant something, and there were those who would no doubt call him a chosen one, Stretch knew the value of humility and invisibility, the seeing and the believing, the vibrations that merged the sciences and the arts, philosophy and religion. Above all, he knew the importance of alignment, the need for acceptance.

For the next three hours he trawled the stages of his lives both physical and spiritual, remembering those who had designed and built and taught and influenced. At the end of this period, he was no longer alone, Sandra wrapping an arm around his shoulders and pulling him close, cradling his remains in her arms, a skeleton no longer needed, mere bone and titanium, and he was with her as she entered her spaceship, accepting that she knew best, feeling the care of her crew and repenting, and when the hatch closed and he was inside familiar surroundings he was thrilled by the beauty of the miraculous as they blasted off and left the crater behind.

The spaceship slipped through the planet's shell and the same sparks appeared and great waves of psychedelia flowed and filled the hollow and ran through the dust and into the rock causing the marble to re-form and the diamonds to return and hold the light of three suns because this was a sacred site and the paradise built by Stretch had been saved so peace could reign here forever and he remained focused on the ship until it was another white light in the heavens a travelling star a meteor carrying that other part of him home for a proper burial leaving his soul to prepare for next Sunday when he would dress in his Best and board the train and travel into the hills and pass through the right gate and proceed along the corridor and enter the valley where his family was waiting for him running to greet their husband father son brother the adventurer uncoiled he had discovered water and life and its myriad realities God and the gods he was honest and decent deserved the ecstasy of the eternal as more loving arms were wrapped around Stretch hugging him tight as tight could be.

Granny's Letters

Granny Smith sat in her armchair listening to the sound of snowflakes on the window, the cushioned blows reminding her of the patter Alan's gloves made that first time she saw him, when he was boxing for his unit. A crowd of soldiers stood in near-silence as they watched the two men dance across the canvas, and while she'd been impressed by their easy movement it was the noise that left the biggest impression. Soft, but sharp. Fresh, clean breaths. Alan was young, strong, alive. The fight had a dignity she hadn't expected. Time slowed and he was illuminated by a ray of brilliant white light. A projector ticked. His face flickering in a series of frames. And then the brightness of the film dipped and he was fading. The picture stuttered. Shadow closed in. She heard him wheeze. Her husband was old and sick and turning into a ghost. He was struggling to breathe. So was Granny. She shut her eyes and shook her head hard, like her and Glad used to do when they were little girls, forcing herself back towards the sound of the snow.

She wasn't Granny in those days of course, but Vi Stevens, a fun-loving eighteen-year-old nurse asked to help the doctor in case one of the boxers was injured. Sweat soaked Alan's body, but she was focusing on his face as he fought, surprised to see how much it contorted when he delivered or took a punch, concentration intensifying his features as he was preparing to attack his opponent or defend himself. It was impossible to know how badly the blows hurt, but she was sure he couldn't be scared as he kept bouncing back, brave and determined, blood smearing his mouth. When he knocked the other lad down in the fourth round the referee stopped the fight and lifted Alan's arm into the air. He was the winner. Vi was thrilled. Her body trembled.

She was young and impulsive and while attending to his cut lip asked him to take her to the pictures in a pretty direct sort of way, while she was using cotton wool to soak up the blood and leaning in close enough so only Alan could hear. The doctor decided the wound didn't need stitches, but it took a long time to mend and left a scar behind. She'd wanted to run her fingers through his light brown hair, loved the hints of red and the smell of his bruised body after he'd dried his skin with a towel, but knew enough to behave like a lady.

They'd gone to see *There Ain't No Justice* at the cinema, based on a novel by her favourite author, James Curtis. The film wasn't as gritty as the book, which was modern and realistic and talked about the sort of subjects movies couldn't in those days, and yet she had loved it all the same. Mind you, not many writers were as daring as Curtis. He used the sort of language she knew, captured the conversations and slang of ordinary Londoners, and it was exciting to see her world in print. His stories were fast-paced and moral, and she developed a bond with this author and his work.

The hero of *There Ain't No Justice* was Tommy Mutch, his role played by Jimmy Hanley who went on to appear in the adaptation of Arthur La Bern's *It Always Rains On Sunday* after the war, one of the best of the Ealing films, and Vi couldn't help herself comparing Hanley to Alan. Tommy was a promising young fighter, headstrong and honest, boxing offering him a way out of poverty, but he was put under pressure to throw a fight. The book was based in the slum of Notting Dale and around nearby Shepherd's Bush, and being an Acton girl Vi knew the locations. It was clear that Curtis was familiar with this part of West London and she wondered if she'd maybe been in the same pub as him and not even known. She could have walked past him in the street, stood at the same stall in the market maybe.

Life was like that... passed you by if you didn't know what was going on under your nose... passed you by if you didn't do something about it when you did know... and so sitting in the Odeon she'd pretended to feel faint, slumped against her boy soldier for support. Alan got the message. Wrapped his right arm around her shoulders.

When he went off to the war she sobbed her heart out, certain she would never see him again, but Alan wrote right away and she replied and they soon had a correspondence going. She was thinking about his letters so much at work that it was hard to concentrate on what she was doing, running over his words again and again so they spiralled away and formed new stories that she guided for a while before letting them loose and seeing where they ended up, and then when she got home she would rush to read the last letter to remind herself of what was true and what was not. She did this with the films she saw and the books she took out of the library, blending them in with reality, but in those days she was always able to remember what went where. Life was like a finished novel, a film that hadn't been shot yet, a series of short stories that needed to connect, and she could make every ending a happy one if she was just alert enough to spot danger and stamp it out.

Waiting for each new letter increased the strain. She tried to guess what it would say, excited and nervous and finally relieved, slicing the envelope open with her grandmother's six-inch hatpin, a sharpened blade she stabbed into a man one night in the West End, after he mistook her for a tart as she was passing the end of Lisle Street. He followed Vi and wouldn't take no for an answer, pushed her into a doorway, and so she stuck the steel in deep, moved it left and right, heard him beg before she pulled the pin out and walked off, leaving her attacker on the ground. Yes, she loved Alan's rounded text with its smooth loops and circled dots, the way the ink flowed black like blood. Vi had been ecstatic as she cut into Leicester Square, reached the tube and trotted down into the depths of London, drained but content by the time she arrived home. At work the next day her worry returned, but for a while she had felt invincible.

When the war ended and Alan came home he took advantage of the courses offered to demobbed soldiers, studied mechanical drawing in the evenings and worked in a garage by day, eventually found a job as a trainee draughtsman, and by his late thirties was making a good living. He carried none of the rage that saw some servicemen turn to drink and violence and crime, though there was a period when he had struggled, thrashing about in his sleep, swearing and shouting his head off in the dark of early morning. Vi would wake him when it became especially bad and glimpsed his terror, watching relief turn to shame, his body drenched in sweat the same as that first time she'd seen him in the boxing ring.

The smell of his nightmares was very different. There was nothing noble about these dreams. His sweat was dirty and soaked the sheets, and then one night he wet the bed. She hadn't known what to do. He was fast asleep, jolting as if he was being electrocuted, and she'd wanted to wake him up but knew he couldn't know what he'd done. It would have destroyed him. Things were different in those days. Men had to behave in certain ways and Vi expected him to be strong, even though as a nurse she had more empathy than most. She knew enough not to be upset by the mess. It was his mental state that worried her as there was no way of knowing what he had experienced. Alan would never tell her and she was never going to ask. Yet it was clearly something terrible. Vi sat there in bed thinking hard and when it was time to get up she brought him a cup of lukewarm tea and pretended to slip and spilled it over the wet sheets – by accident... on purpose. The trick worked.

Looking back, Violet was sure he'd never guessed the truth. All these years later she was seeing him stumble away to wash and get ready for work, saw herself stripping the mattress and coming home from the hospital at dinnertime and scrubbing the sheets in the sink and hanging them out in the drizzle to remove the smell. Alan already felt bad about shouting in his sleep, part of a generation determined to control its fears and look to the future. And she was Vi again, sitting in those dirty bedclothes listening to the rain hammer on the roof, worrying about the water leaking through the rotting wood of the window frames. But whenever Alan woke from a nightmare she was there to cuddle him like he was a child, reassuring and making him strong again, and sometimes she would wait until he was calm and go down between his legs and make him hard with her mouth and get on top and ride him until she came and he filled her up. There were lots of good times. Some great memories. They fucked like rabbits. That's what Alan used to say. It was rare for him to swear. Granny blushed and Violet grinned and Vi stuck her tongue out.

Boxing helped Alan through his nightmares. Vi and the boxing... After demob he joined a club in Shepherd's Bush and trained for five or six years, maintaining his fitness and discipline and ridding himself of his anger on a punchbag. He sparred, but never fought in a proper contest. When he was away in the army, Vi would make up stories where Alan starred, imagined him as Tommy Mutch for a while but preferred something a bit different, stuck him in the role of Shorty Mathews, hero of another Curtis novel *They Drive By Night*.

Released from Pentonville as a man was about to be hanged inside the prison walls, one of the first things Shorty did was visit a girlfriend who also happened to be a prostitute. Finding her murdered, he was sure that as an ex-con he would be accused of the crime, convicted and executed, so he went on the run, left London and hitched rides on the Great North Road. Dodging the police, he ended up saving a girl who was about to be raped, while the real murderer turned out to be a serial killer from Clapham Junction, a lunatic who'd been attacking streetwalkers in the West End. Ernest Thesiger played the part so well he terrified Vi when she watched the film. Thesiger was the creepiest murderer she'd ever seen. Justice was done. The killer was caught and Shorty survived.

Curtis wrote five novels before the war and she had read them all, but then he seemed to disappear. Recently she'd found out he only had one more book published, dying poor and alone in Kilburn, drinking too much in the local pubs, probably disappointed by life. To have such ability and see it stifled was tragic. She wondered what had happened, but those five novels had made her think about life in a different way. Curtis took her into the clubs of Soho in *The Gilt Kid*, on the road with girls who had sex with lorry drivers in return for lifts in *They Drive By Night*, and into the boxing world with *There Ain't No Justice*. There were plenty of crooks about, but each book looked at the struggles of working people, the unfairness in society. Violet thought about Tommy Mutch's sister and the abortion and how it went wrong, the girl dying along with her child, and Violet's chest heaved as she imagined Vi in the same situation, had to remind herself that it was the story of an imaginary girl in a forgotten book. Thesiger stalked her near Lisle Street. She stabbed him and made the monster squeal, didn't care if he lived or died. Sometimes there *was* justice.

Her reality was a long marriage that had been near enough perfect. They'd been blessed with two healthy children, unlike poor Glad whose boy Freddie passed away before he was two years old, his death changing her sister forever. He was their only child and Gladys separated from her husband Bob soon after. She had suffered from bouts of depression ever since. Living alone hadn't helped. Each day Violet looked at her life and marvelled at how lucky she'd been. The time they'd had together before Alan went off to fight Hitler made them closer than most of those who met after the war, and their letters bonded them so tightly they were never going to break up in peacetime. He hadn't written again, and she used to tell him a letter was long overdue, as she was sure he had a special way with words, even if he was a quiet man and they were buried deep inside his head. In another existence he might have been an author, but times were hard and he had to earn a living. It was a different sort of existence. Special in its own unique way.

Before, during and just after the war they would drink too much and go dancing and have sex in parks and doorways and once on the top deck of an empty bus, but they had survived the bombing and the fighting overseas and were grateful. They'd never taken anything for granted. It was important to stand on your own two feet and not blame others for your mistakes. People talked themselves up rather than down. They had very little and refused handouts. There were rules and you minded your own business, but they were proud people and she remembered more laughter in those days. Maybe she was wrong. Even so, she pitied the young girls today, lacking privacy and unable to say what they thought, many of them in terrible debt, the rights her generation had fought so hard for quietly stripped away.

More than anything else, she'd known fear when she was young. Alan prayed he wouldn't be sent to the Far East, whispering that he didn't want to die in a jungle, more scared of snakes and malaria than the bloody Japs. He had ended up fighting in North Africa and Italy with the 8th Army, part of Operations Crusader and Husky. Later he would talk about them going to Sicily one day, struck by the beauty of the place, but they never had that sort of money and there were the children to think about. It would have been nice to have lived abroad for a while, especially when they were older and the cold got inside their bones, but it didn't happen. She had never been out of England, apart from a couple of holidays in Wales. Not that she was complaining.

She did miss that older English culture though. They had voted for a fresh start after the war and the welfare state was born and she was proud to be part of the NHS. There was an ongoing battle with the rich, but she had a side and did her best. The enemy was still out there, but people didn't seem to realise what was going on now. Alan wasn't political like Vi, but he knew the score. Most people were okay once you got to know them, and at least your enemies were easy to spot. Those war years and the immediate aftermath had been the best time of her life, and yet she felt terrible thinking this way, knew how lucky she'd been to live in Britain. She had tried to put herself in the position of a mother in a concentration camp, holding her child, about to be gassed, but it was impossible. How could humans do that to each other? It was beyond belief. The decades passed and Violet Smith counted her blessings.

When Alan died she thought she was going to go mad. It was nearly four years ago... She ran a finger along that scar on his mouth as she sat with the body. Tidied his grey hair with a comb, the red faded to grey along with the brown. When she finally left the ward Violet collapsed in the hospital car park. The children tried to comfort her in the weeks that followed, and the grandkids offered new life, but nobody could know how she felt. They mourned their father and grandfather, but had never known Alan in the same way. He was her lover, friend, husband. They were young and full of hope and suddenly he was middle-aged and slowing down, ageing too fast, finally sick and older than his years and suffering and trying to hide his fear. She had seen him take punches and go back for more, refusing to surrender, and blamed the war for his illness. And then Alan was gone. Vi died with him and Violet shuffled into the darkness. Granny roamed the bungalow and its garden and sat in her armchair by the window and watched the empty street and was lost.

It was Gladys who came to the rescue. She had stopped Granny killing herself. Glad with her years of sadness, living two hundred miles away and talking on the phone but more importantly writing those long letters that Granny read and read and watched for every day. Gladys carried her through all sorts of emotions, expressing the loneliness she now felt, the anger and resentment, an incredible emptiness, and then Glad would pull her up with childhood memories and her views on the funny repetitions and contradictions of life. Glad's words charged across the paper, digging into the pulp, a series of jagged edges and vicious hooks, feelings easier to express with a pen. Violet returned.

Gladys' letters always ended optimistically, and she demanded quick replies, which Violet immersed herself in writing, and it was only recently that she realised how the correspondence had probably helped her sister as well. They wrote all the time these days, back and forwards, were closer than they'd ever been. Violet made an effort with her style, thought about what she was going to say for a day or two, eager to get the right words out. It would never be the same without Alan, but after a year she was able to embrace her Granny Smith role with the kids – *she was Violet,* Granny was an invention – and looked forward to their visits, telling them stories she made up in the moment. They wanted her to write them down, but she felt silly, said they weren't very good, and then when they kept on she told them she'd think about it, but only to stop them asking. She was no writer. The very idea…

Her oldest grandchild was Millie and she came round twice a week. They were easy in each other's company. Granny made the girl her favourite foods. Millie was shy and self-conscious, drifted and flickered – like Alan in some ways – as small as he had been big, but she was secretly strong and sure to gain in confidence. Millie had seen spirits when she was little, something the doctors said would pass, while Granny had hoped it never would. She'd been the same, wished she still had the gift, but it faded away when she was eight or so, which was a shame. Millie was fourteen now and Granny and Violet wanted to ask her questions, but held back. Everyone needed privacy. Vi was nagging them though, wanted to know if Alan was still alive, when he was coming home, but she was young and impatient, had to learn to stay calm and control her bloody temper.

Granny only really became angry when she let herself focus on how that post-war idealism had been attacked and undermined, the sacrifices made increasingly meaningless as today's career politicians allowed everything of value be sold off to the highest bidders. Privatisation had handed essential services to profit-driven companies that didn't care about people or genuine communities. When she thought of how Britain had been betrayed she despaired, and when she tried to talk about these things to her children they just nodded and smiled and seemed bored. This was hard for her to accept. They told her the world had changed, but what did that mean? The same problems existed. Writing to Glad let Violet express her feelings, but she didn't go on too much, didn't want to be seen as a moaner. She wondered how Gladys would reply to her last letter.

Violet normally sensed the postman approaching, and when she saw him walking down the road she would wait to see if he turned towards her front door, disappointed when he kept going, excited if he came down the path. Apart from the bills and junk mail, she received a letter a week from Gladys and five or six each year from her brother in Canada. Sometimes there was news from friends who had moved away, a holiday postcard now and then. She kept her correspondences going, enjoyed the choosing of paper and envelopes, the writing and sealing and attaching of stamps and even the posting. Most of all she loved the thinking involved. It made her a part of the world.

Granny reached for her tea. She held the cup firmly between both hands to avoid spilling it down her front. The brew felt good in her mouth, soothing but also refreshing. Replacing the cup on the side table she pushed herself up out of the chair and took a couple of steps so she could touch the window and feel its coldness, noticed how the buildings and cars and gardens were turning into a collage, a series of cutouts that made her think of Matisse and the scissors he used as an elderly man, and she jolted, remembered those letters she'd received when she was in her late-thirties, newsprint stuck down with glue to form dirty words and a story and a threat. First-class stamps. It was impossible. Alan would never do such a thing. He was honest. Like the boxer Tommy Mutch.

Snowflakes settled on the window, lasted a few seconds before fading away like the boxers and soldiers and writers and husbands and children and the few bad memories she carried and her private secrets and the sort of man who was threatening to damage her family. She wished she had a microscope. No two flakes were ever identical. There was a spread she'd pulled out of a magazine that showed fifty of them in close-up, and while they looked as if they were made of steel and straight out of a factory, each snowflake was unique.

The clouds were hanging lower in the sky and the snow was thickening. The sound on the glass was becoming louder and more intense, and there was this other film she'd seen, about a blackmailer who demanded sex to keep his mouth shut. The cinema cheered as he was repeatedly stabbed. Or maybe his killing came from the pages of a book. She wasn't sure. Even though her favourite author dealt in justice, this one had nothing to do with James Curtis. Granny and Violet watched Vi getting dressed, tarting herself up, slipping a kitchen knife into her handbag when she was ready, right next to their gran's hatpin. It was a modern film. Violent and frenzied.

Full colour. The police said it was a brutal attack. Multiple stab wounds. The old black-and-white movies were better.

Granny watched the news on television and tried to work out what was happening with the Post Office, saw that a combination of Tory and EU ideology was threatening its break-up and privatisation. Really it needed to be protected, expanded and properly subsidised, and with the increase in packages through internet selling and the need for a people's bank it could be booming. She had memories and knowledge to pass on. It was frustrating that she couldn't do this, but she refused to give up like so many elderly people did. An NHS nurse, she had lived a worthwhile life and hoped she'd made a difference. She still had so much to offer. Just wanted to help.

She looked at the small clock she kept nearby. The postman was nearly an hour late. Frank was a young lad, maybe twenty-five, rushing around to deal with larger workload he'd been forced to take on, always said hello and stopped for a chat when the weather was good and she was out in the front garden and he wasn't running late. Violet had been a union rep for the last sixteen years of her working life and always asked him about what was going on, and he explained the workings better than any reporter. And then he was gone. Under pressure. In a rush. The post only came once a day now instead of twice, and her local post office had been closed down eighteen months before.

Maybe they really would decide that the people who lived round this way weren't worth the bother. Perhaps the letters would stop. It was hard to believe, seeing as everyone got old eventually – if they were lucky – and yet the elderly were being marginalised, politicians talking about the cost of their healthcare as if it was a problem. It was the likes of Alan and her who had paid for the system their entire working lives. They had been there at the start. It wasn't fair.

Only last week there had been a discussion on the radio where one of these so-called experts argued that the NHS should be privatised. Violet pursed her lips. It needed investment, that was all, but the NHS was safe. People would never stand by and let it be broken up. It was the same with the post office and the libraries that had lent her so many books to read. Big business needed constant change, hated a history that created pride and unity. The robots in charge laughed at sentimentality but were unnerved by it, knew that emotion was a threat to their sterile profit motive. But nobody she knew wanted to hear Granny Smith talking about these things. She was the past. If it wasn't for the letters the postman delivered she could have died years ago and never even realised.

Granny rested her forehead on Violet's reflection. The glass was icy cold and she used it to revive herself. She was getting in a tizzy for no good reason. This could happen when you lived alone. The letters would never stop coming. It was important to stay strong and fight the loneliness, but there were times when it was overwhelming. She stood back and shook her head hard again, forcing herself to refocus and appreciate how the snow was starting to stick to the glass for longer, trying to hold on and live forever. She let the sound take her back to the side of that ring where two young men were trading a flurry of punches. Her body shook. The veins in her arms and legs and head and chest were burning. The fight was over and the boxers shook hands. Respect flowed through the hall and out into the world beyond. Every single person mattered. She was strong again.

The postman was late, but it was the weather responsible. She didn't want Frank to rush and slip in the snow and hurt himself, break an arm or a leg, bruise his body, end up with a cut mouth. Still, she hoped he got here soon as Vi was expecting a letter from Alan and was very excited, while Violet knew Gladys was writing with a moving-in date. The sisters were going to live together. They were looking forward to the future. Granny Smith scanned the street outside. Her face was one big smile. She was optimistic. They were going to be happy. But it was best that the postman took his time.

See No Evil

The room was clean and simple and big for a man on his own, for someone straight out of prison, for the likes of Jimmy Ramone. Pausing inside the open door he admired the single bed with its brown blanket and green pillows, the metal desk and wicker chair, an empty vase, the sagging old armchair soaked in millions of halfway-house dreams. There was a large painting on the widest wall and he went across for a closer look, making sure he clicked the door shut first. Black-ink monkeys moved through overgrown ruins. Broken bricks poked from waves of red and purple and yellow flowers, the stems long, heads nodding. He wondered if his father was alive, if their paths would ever cross. His dad could even have painted this picture. Jimmy's lungs heaved at the idea, but he controlled his breathing, as he'd learned to do in Seven Towers, moved in close and studied the scene.

The flowers were as tall as the monkeys, all but one of these creatures walking upright, a crouched loner dragging balled fists along the ground, broad back hunched against a wobbling sun. Seven monkeys carried seven lengths of wood, and at first he thought these were staffs to help them walk, seeing as the ruins were tumbling down the side of a hill, but they held their stripped branches as if they were clubs, so he supposed he was wrong. He turned away. Inspected the room.

Thick curtains hung either side of a narrow window, offering the sort of privacy it was easy to take for granted outside of prison. He ran his right hand over the glass, pleased it wasn't chipped, cracked, broken. He opened the pane and pushed his head out into the hot evening air, realising as he did so that there were no bars, his freedom floating in a breeze of oranges and lemons. He peered into the narrow street four storeys down, digging back and seeing himself as a boy on an frosty street corner, a shivering kid checking left and right, a youngster with a drink in his hand and a song in his head. He pulled back into the moment, shifted ahead, surfing that flow of perfume. Past, present and future – it was all the same to Jimmy Ramone.

If a man wanted to survive in jail he had to diffuse time, needed to convince himself that his sentence was going to pass quickly, that life on the outside would last a lot longer than the term he was serving. But it was a non-stop battle, so if he was clever, a bit of a philosopher, he could insist that time didn't even exist, because if everything was born to grow and struggle and fade and die then why did any of what was happening to him matter? It was all an illusion. Prison became a monastery, the convict a monk. The right man could have great insights, experience bliss, his spirit breaking free and circling the planet.

If nothing lasted, though, it also followed that every single second was precious, so wasting time was the worst sort of crime. The prisoner started to panic. His heart stuttered, brain crashing as the mania of the block closed in, the violence upsetting him more than usual, the monkey monsters under his bed tracing the outline of his spine with their nails. Childhood terrors returned. A familiar voice tried to help – *go on, stab him, he deserves it, and it'll feel good, trust me, I promise you it will feel so fucking good if you kick and punch and knife one of these dirty funhouse freaks* – but Jimmy resisted the temptation, stayed near his calendar and crossed out numbers, drawing women with curved bodies and lipstick smiles. It was one way of staying in control, but what really kept him going was knowing that when he was released he would never get into trouble again. This was the truth. It was a fact.

He heard footsteps in the street and leaned out of the window again, the sound growing louder, two figures forming and slowing as they approached a neon sign. It was odd. He hadn't noticed this sign before. There was a burst of piano as a boy and girl entered the bar, and he smiled, imagined cold beer being served, could almost taste it, moved back into his room and stood straight, stretching his arms and legs and scanning the walls. He didn't know what to do with himself. It was the first time he'd been alone for two years. He went over to the desk and sat down, started tapping his fingers on the surface. His teeth chattered. Holding his hands up he found that they were trembling. He suddenly felt very cold. This scared him. Men became institutionalised, cracked up when they were released. He might have a fit, fall down and hit his head and die right here, on his own, body incinerated and the ashes scattered by a stranger. Perhaps he would end his own life.

He shook his head, angry at this weakness. He closed his eyes. Somewhere a man spoke, his voice muffled, merging with that of a woman. A radio delivered important news he couldn't understand. The smell of bread made him feel hungry, but he couldn't go out looking for food. Not on his first night of freedom. It was too dangerous. If he could get through the next twelve hours he would be safe. In the morning he would walk to the station without stopping and leave on the first train heading north. All he had to do was stay in this room. The door of the bar creaked loud and he heard a familiar song.

#

Thick walls towered above Jimmy as he turned off the main road and dipped into a side street. He was feeling good, picked out every step, stopped across from the bar and took a few seconds to appreciate the sign's fluorescent wave as it washed into a palm, imagined he was in the tropics, sitting on a beach with a glass of rum in his hand. It was warm enough here, but the tension of the city was tightening, so he knew he couldn't linger, brushed fingers across his forehead and wiped water away, the neon popping and jerking him forward. He reached for the door but it swung open before he touched the handle, a boy and girl hurrying past, heads down and eyes averted. They seemed familiar and he tried to see their faces, but the features were blurred. He went inside.

Music boomed and a spinning fan cooled his skin. The bar was dimly lit and his eyes took a few seconds to adjust, a single beer tap drawing him to the counter. He had sworn he wouldn't touch alcohol tonight, not in this city, not after what happened before, but despite the promise he knew one drink wasn't going to hurt. He would make it last and enjoy the taste alone, then turn around and leave and walk straight back to his room.

The barmaid bent forward and smiled, her low-cut top showing off some fine cleavage. Jimmy pointed to the tap and watched as she poured his drink, bubbles racing up the height of an expanding glass. She fluttered lush eyelashes and licked thick red lips, soaking him in a cloud of perfume. Everything about this lady seemed exaggerated. He was pleased. She placed the glass on the counter and he handed over coins, studying her legs as she went to the till. He glanced along the length of the bar, which was narrow and led to a flickering jukebox, the overall shape of the room reminding him of the section back in prison. Fifteen or so people sat at tables, their heads lowered, while three men in black leather coats stood nearby, talking between themselves.

The barmaid held out his change and made sure their hands touched. He wondered if she knew where he had been, what he had done, if she could see his mistakes in the pallor of his skin, the dull light in his eyes, the colours of his aura, and yet he didn't feel tired or weak or broken, was enjoying the energy racing into his arm, chest, heart. He saw an electric chair, a tethered youth turning into a pig, face glistening, but Jimmy blocked the image out, refused to deal in lies, the casual dismissal of another creature's terror. He was shaking as he returned the barmaid's smile.

Jimmy reached for his glass, determined to sip and enjoy every drop. The barmaid watched closely as he brought the drink to his mouth. He finished his beer in one go and she nodded her approval. It tasted fantastic. He pointed to the tap.

Taking this second glass over to an empty table, Jimmy sat and watched the barmaid stroll down the bar to serve the three men in leather coats. He couldn't work out why they were dressed this way in such warm weather, frustrated he couldn't go over and explain the reality of what they had wrapped around their backs. He wondered if the barmaid understood the terror involved. He felt that she must. And it was fantastic leaving a world of men and being so near a woman, even brushing her hand, but he couldn't let his guard down, remembered the place he'd been drinking in before his arrest, knew the sort of violence that could occur. He would finish this one and leave, the alcohol doing its job, lifting his spirits and numbing any doubts. He was in charge, his old confidence returning. Resting his head against the wall he shut his eyes and concentrated on the jukebox, pictured the B-Block boys, all those convicts who were dreaming their lives away. He said a short prayer for the friends he had left behind.

When he opened his eyes again he found the barmaid staring at him. He realised his glass was empty. He nodded and she poured another, bringing it over on a tray with a big shot of vodka. This was on the house. She eased in close, whispering words he didn't know, a breast brushing his arm. She flicked her tongue and returned to the counter, wiggling her hips as she went, and he flashed back in time, was walking next to Ramona, his soulmate swaying in the same way, but for different reasons. They were two runaways on an iced-up pavement, treading carefully, the gutters heavy with sludge, petrol-grey snow seeping into drains loaded with fermenting hormones. They were approaching a market and it was Jimmy who spotted the police car and guided Ramona into the crowd, over to the nearest shop window. They would look at the display with their backs to the road, wait for the police to move on, their reflections distorted in the wet glass.

A single face formed and stared back. It had huge ears, a massive snout and delicate eyelids that sagged over empty sockets. The eyes had been burned or scooped out, or maybe they had just decayed. Blood crusted what remained of the neck, rubber-skin rigid where it had been hacked at by a blade. Ramona slumped forward and Jimmy just caught her in time, before she shattered the window, holding on until she was able to drive some strength back into her legs. Ramona mumbled and Jimmy thought he was going to be sick, held the nausea down, turned his head and saw two policemen standing by their car, scanning the crowd. He returned to the pig, felt its fear, heard the screaming of its slaughter, and his disgust rose up again, nearly reached his mouth, and what made the murder and mutilation even more perverted was the pig's smile. It wasn't a modest grin or a cheeky little smirk, but a great big lucky-me-isn't-life-fantastic beam.

Jimmy waited a while before looking round again, and when he did the police were gone. He tugged Ramona away from the glass, hurrying them as best he could towards the pub at the end of the road. They passed stalls loaded with nuts and bolts and old clothes, the fruit-and-veg men with their oranges and lemons, the roast-chestnut lady poking at grey coals, a range of secondhand radios and televisions and broken neons, a bakery selling fresh bread and pies. They turned into a narrow little street and were soon pushing the pub door open, warm air cushioning their entrance. An elderly couple were leaving a table and Ramona flopped into one of the seats, the woman patting her shoulder softly, their faces lost as they went out into the cold.

Jimmy stood tall at the counter and ordered. He was under-age but nobody cared. Three leather-coated men stood on one side, four market traders on the other. The barmaid smiled at him as she poured beer, those near him admiring her cleavage. Jimmy glanced around the pub, saw loners and couples keeping to themselves, a selection of grafters and shoppers and music-lovers talking and arguing and laughing, and then he could hear their hearts inside a jukebox that thumped out punk and rockabilly and some vintage rock n roll. Smoke filled the air, lyrics lost in the din.

He brought their drinks over to the table and joined Ramona, who grabbed his hands and rubbed hard to warm them up. This was the free world at its best – a warm pub and good beer, the chance to say what he thought, a beautiful girl who was moral and smart, the record-machine and its 45s. They guzzled stout and lager, slowly calming down, even if Jimmy couldn't stop thinking ahead. They would have to move on soon. If the police found them they would be split up and he would be sent back to the home. One more after this and then they would leave. They had to keep their heads down and stay out of trouble.

Years later and straight out of prison, Jimmy had plans. Tomorrow morning he would be sitting on a train, but tonight he could relax and listen to the songs and enjoy the barmaid's smile. He kept on drinking, toasted Ramona and that nameless pig. Prison could shock even the hardest of men, make them examine themselves and question the peck-peck-pecking order, and he thought of the animals on the work farm, the men who refused to take part in the killing. There were no release dates in the slaughterhouse. No escape and no mercy shown to the meek. He had seen the horror with his own eyes. He would never forget the cruelty of the knackers. His mood changed.

He wondered what these people in the bar would think if they knew he had just been released from Seven Towers. Some might call him an animal, but they would really mean subhuman. Others might see him as a novelty. He tried to guess which men would pick a fight, settled his eyes on the barmaid and tried to decide if she would be disgusted or excited. It would be better if she was sympathetic. He hunched over his glass. There were some truly honest people in the world, but not so many. Ramona was the best he'd ever known.

He saw them in that market pub, drinking too much and staying too long, going back out into the winter cold, careful as they headed towards the station, trying not to skid and fall. The buildings were trimmed with ice and the streetlights reflected at odd angles, and as they passed through this fluorescent corridor they neared the butcher's shop. He had looked across the road, seen the pig's head in the window, and it was glowing and cartoon-like and the two beasts behind the counter were laughing, making more noise that the whole of the pub put together. One man held a cleaver. There was a poster advertising chops. A smiling lamb frolicked in a green field.

The market was closing and rubbish was being collected. Jimmy reached into a skip and took out a lump of wood, crossed through the barely moving traffic and reached the window, whacked the glass one, two, three, four times before it exploded. He shouted at Ramona to run as the butchers stepped forward, blades in their hands, white overalls red with blood, using some of their cheerful slaughterhouse chat – *come here you little bastard, I'm going to cut your balls off* – because that's how these people talked and thought and lived their lives, but they were fat and stunk of another creature's death and Jimmy had a head start, one of the men slipping on the ice, the boy stopping and shouting, the second butcher near when Jimmy tumbled and fell, hauling himself back up and reaching Ramona who couldn't move as fast, and the butcher was right behind them now, Jimmy stopping to face him, running forward and cracking him on the head and watching the body collapse, hitting him three more times.

Jimmy and Ramona reached the station and trotted down the escalators. They jumped on the first train they saw and rubbed noses as the doors closed.

He couldn't help feeling pleased. He had never known how to behave himself. He was different now and one day he would find Ramona. They thought the same way, used to worry about the dairy cows, all those mothers mourning sons snatched and sent off to veal factories, their daughters raped and filled with drugs, jolly farmers castrating the boys and fingering the girls so the eyes of the innocents widened in shock and embarrassment. He hated the advertising whores and dishonest journalists who pumped out snide humour to hide the horror;

the politicians and religious leaders who allowed the killing to continue and increase. Ramona cried for the scared chicks and lambs and piglets and all the innocent creatures of the world, while Jimmy raged about those responsible. The masses turned their heads and refused to see the real criminals. He hated the hypocrites who sneered and dismissed and judged. Prison had reinforced and focused his beliefs.

The jukebox was silent and he realised he was on his feet and walking over. He had been in the bar for a couple of hours and his mind was marching in a different directions. He bumped into one of the men at the bar, commented on the leather coat.

Jimmy stood in front of the machine and looked at the records – inspecting them as a man and a boy – in a foreign bar and a local pub – and the drink had hit him harder than he'd expected. He was starting to drift. Ramona and him were the only ones on this dirty planet who could hear the muttering of the meat men, the snickering of their child-molester bosses, the oohing and aahing of the fashion pedophiles in their fur and stripped skin, the great leather-buying, burger-gorging, baby-battering, tastebud-driven public. His head was spinning. He could see those meekest of souls in the slaughterhouse – lambs and piglets and calves crying for their mothers – and he felt their panic as they faced the horror, the last words these creatures heard the swearing of evil men heavy with the sex of their razors and hooks and drills and knives – angry swearing grunting rapist laughter – *dirty little bitch shitting on my boots... go on, stick that electric rod up her, that'll make her eyes water... look at him trying to hide his face, come on, cut his bollocks off* – and he could feel the fear of the section... the anger of the prison house... as if he was still locked-up... he could hear the mutter of the other men... the jabbering... the peck-peck-pecking of the pecking order... the tick-tick-ticking... and he saw the judges in their finery... the pontificators... the snobs and liars... knew he was judging them as well... but there *was* a difference... the difference between right and wrong... good and evil... there *had* to be a difference... life wouldn't make sense otherwise... there were plenty in prison who deserved to be shut away... but there were more lost boys and innocents than evil men... they had made mistakes... he had made enough in his life... but he wasn't bad... hadn't done anything wrong... not really... just a fight after too much drink... it was easily done... a way to release his fury... and he turned and saw the three leathermen standing close... sneering... glaring... snarling... cocky there in their black coats... so Jimmy moved away from the jukebox and faced them and hardened his fists.

#

The room was simple and dirty and small for someone who had tasted freedom, for Jimmy Ramone pressing his head against the bars that filled one end of the barren cell. It was similar to the place they had held him in two years ago, before he was sent up the hill to Seven Towers. The smell was identical, a sour blend of sweat, piss, shit, vomit, fear. The stench of the prison house was even worse, these essentials drenched in the sheer insanity of incarceration, a rancid brand of failure that promised cancer, heart failure, clots, brain damage and every sort of infection and virus. It was also the smell of a hospital, but without the detergent and decency.

Bleached hospital corridors pulled visitors to the hopelessness of a ward lined with the elderly, a hall of memories, regrets, visions, nightmares, exhaustion. Morphine was a true friend, an angel of mercy offering sedation, silence, a drifting mental calm. Time turned full circle, moving from the wonders of potty training to the final release of incontinence. This was the place where the fears of Jimmy's prison philosophy came true. Time ran out. There was no going back, no second or third or tenth chances. Ward 6 was waiting for every man, woman, boy, girl. A single second was precious. There were never enough seconds, minutes, hours, days, weeks, months, years. Time was everything. He squeezed the bars.

What had he done?

What the fuck had he done to end up in this cell?

Thinking back a few hours...

He should have stayed in his room.

Jimmy felt the cuts on his knuckles, bruised eyes looking for a human face, but there was nobody in the corridor and he was the only one in the cell. The guards were around the corner, out of sight, drinking tea and playing cards. The ice-cream man didn't visit any more. He was dead. Stabbed to death in a prison toilet. That's what Jimmy had heard. What he had seen.

He shut his eyes.

Butted the bars.

Felt blood drop down his face.

#

Excited people filled the train station, pushing past the friendly stranger leaning against a wall, doing his best to blend in. He wanted to remain anonymous, maybe release small sparks of blue-tinted kindness, the sort of colours a sensitive soul would understand. He was living the lessons of the prison yard and protecting his back, wary of knitting needles that punctured lungs, shards of glass that sliced skin and opened arteries, fingernails that ripped at a sleeping man's spine. He was ready for the back-stabbers prowling the train stations and bus depots of the world, the street-corner snipers waiting for drunks and drifters. He was a transient himself, so knew the reality. He was also a lucky man, arrested on his first night of freedom for being drunk and asleep in a doorway, the police releasing him in the morning with a cheerful warning, unaware of his past.

Jimmy saw animals crowd the platform, identified vegan sniffers and snorters, the happy faces of pigs and cows and sheep and rabbits and mice and geese and a single carrot-chomping donkey. This was a world where simple manners masked a different sort of knowledge. He was one of only a few humans who could see this bully-free alternative, but he noticed he was giggling, raised a hand to cover his mouth as a grandmother glared over, her eyes narrowing as an arm instinctively reached towards the two little girls by her side. The arm floated, holding his future in the balance, and when she lowered it and turned away and dismissed the idea of danger Jimmy felt fantastic.

His train arrived and he found a seat by the window. An elderly man sat opposite. The face was mean and pinched and cruel, but when a cloud shunted sideways and sunlight filled the carriage the expression was almost saintly. Big ears protruded from the skull. A sign of wisdom. And they seemed to be growing. The shape of the head was also changing, wrinkles vanishing as the skin became smooth and very clean. Jimmy had always liked pigs. The nose was filling out and stretching and turning into a rubber snout. It wasn't long before a beaming porker sat across from him, but Jimmy frowned, wondered if it was a trick, if he was refusing to see the evil. This was something he had learned to do as a boy, but that skill was meant to have been left in the past, and yet the past was right here in the present, and this exact moment was waiting in the future. He pulled himself together. The man's features returned. He seemed worried and Jimmy realised he had been pulling some faces of his own. The train was moving. They had already left the station behind. Jimmy nodded and smiled.

The old man meant no harm and seemed relieved, pulled a small table down and dipped into the sack sitting on his knees, taking out a bottle and two shot glasses. One hand made flamboyant gestures as the other conjured bags of raisins, pumpkin seeds, radishes, almonds. He tore each one so the contents spilled across the table. Next he produced a thick loaf of bread, finally unscrewing the top of the bottle and filling the glasses with a mystery spirit. He handed one of these to Jimmy. The man said a few words and they drank a toast. The spirit stung Jimmy's throat. It was powerful stuff. They had two more glasses and settled back in their seats.

Fields had replaced the last suburbs of the city and the train was crossing scrubland, the earth dry and dusty, a lone donkey chained to a rock in the full glare of a fast-rising sun.

Jimmy could feel its heartbeat inside his own chest. There was no music. No jukebox. His mouth was suddenly dry. Eyes wet. He tried to push the donkey from his mind, concentrating on the forest ahead of the train. This was a sanctuary for runaways. His relief at finally escaping the city and heading north clashed with the anger he felt, the train picking up speed. But nothing could stop him now. He was free.

The man opposite lifted almonds and raisins to his mouth and began chewing, jaw moving slowly with a faint crunch of bone, slipped his hand back into the sack, and Jimmy wiped the tears away and blinked and focused and frowned and hoped that – *for his sake* – he didn't pull out a block of cheese or a stack of sliced ham or a lump of pork.

Jimmy closed his eyes and did his best to lose himself in the motion of the train, searching for the sort of rhythm that would calm his fear and rage and make sure he stayed safe. But he was finding it hard to concentrate, couldn't shut out the click-click-clicking of a meat-eater's teeth. He pushed his thoughts towards the beauty of that simple, private room instead, tried to examine the painting on the wall. The watercolour was wet and had run. And he could hear the tap-tap-tapping of monkey monsters under his bed. The tick-tick-ticking of the time bomb inside his head. He kept his eyes firmly shut, terrified of what he would find when he opened them again.

Writing The Canals

In the second half of the Sixties, we lived in a ground-floor maisonette on the Oxford Road in Denham, next to Uxbridge on the edge of West London, the six lanes outside split by a slender strip of concrete where we would sometimes run with Mum or Dad during a lull in the traffic, balancing there as the lorries barrelled past inches from our heads, waiting for another gap to appear before hurrying to the other side to see our friends. This A road was as wide and busy as the motorways that would soon spread across the country, and in time the M40 and M4 would connect via the M25 locally, adding more layers to the routes in and out of London, each one marking an era and the changing pace of life.

During the busier periods, the glass rattled inside the metal frames of our windows, although being a child with childish things on my mind I don't remember this, but I *do* remember the peace that engulfed us when we went out to play, walking away from the Oxford Road down Cheapside Lane and into the village. A sleepy old street of terraced cottages, there were two pubs and a church, a hidden manor house at one end, a mucky farm at the other. And what I remember even more than *this* are the fields and especially the canal beyond. This was an isolated place, and we weren't meant to go there without an adult, but of course we sometimes did.

With the Oxford Road's fumes merging with the summertime pong of the manured council smallholdings across from the maisonette, the highway's dirty modernism was another world away from the canal and its surroundings. The water was silent, still and empty, running in a dead straight line in either direction, suggesting exotic locations and all sorts of adventures. I don't recall many narrowboats or barges, and the canal felt forgotten along with the fields, which in truth were left to grow until it was time to cut the hay. It was as if we had stepped through a hole in time, which in some ways I suppose we had.

This stretch of the Grand Union runs out from Uxbridge to Birmingham and the Midlands, and its star was and remains a small humpback footbridge. I would also visit the canal with my dad and sister, taking our fishing net along to try and catch a tiddler. We always ended up in the middle of what we knew as the White Bridge, where I stood on tiptoes to see over the wall. We stayed there for ages, like kings of the castle, before walking further out towards Harefield. There was a lock where we would stop, and I must have seen a lot of narrowboats there as I was amazed at the size of the gates, the mechanics involved in opening and closing them, how the water rose and fell, and the thrill of seeing one of these inventions in action has never left me, along with the belief that being a lock-keeper living in a house by the canal must be one of the best jobs in the world. Along with being a writer.

These were simple pleasures, shared by many thousands of people, true, but while my memories may not be over-detailed, they remain firm, loaded with romance and even mystery, and those ideas of what the canals represent, notions of parallel journeys and the passage of time, have fermented in my subconscious over the years, re-emerging in several of my novels.

By the start of the 1970s we had moved to nearby Iver Heath, between Uxbridge and Slough, a couple of miles each way on a London Country bus, and the latter was where I went to school and spent a lot of time in the coming years. I would regularly cross the Slough Arm of the Grand Union where it flanks the Great Western Railway tracks linking Paddington to the West Country and South Wales, the two bridges following in quick succession, passing the gasworks and a mosque, in those days coming to the greyhound stadium where Slough Town played their football, next to the A4, a little further on the M4. Canal, railway, road, motorway… Horses, steam, the internal combustion engine…

This was my home, the outer London limits where the urban meets the rural, and running through our lives were those parallel paths and periods, a tiering of the ages captured in the movement of goods, sometimes at the fore of our thinking, always in the background. The Slough Arm was very different to the White Bridge stretch, the section leading away from the gasworks to the dead end at Slough Basin thick with vegetation and rubbish. I didn't walk out the other way until years later, but it seems that would have been the same, a truly abandoned area that in its heyday had been boomed with labour and importance.

Built in 1882, and coming off the Grand Union at Cowley Peachey Junction, the Slough Arm serviced the Iver brickworks, with barges bringing the materials needed to make the bricks, along with refuse to be dumped in the hollows left by local clay and gravel excavations, plus horse manure for the fields. These barges then returned to the Paddington Basin loaded with the building blocks of London's expansion. I know this part of the Slough Arm now, and the remains of the brickworks are buried in the undergrowth. It is hard to grasp how big the workforce must have been, with Iver boasting a lot more pubs than it does today.

When I was old enough to drink, we would often head to a canalside pub, especially in the summer, and a couple of these were magically named the Malt Shovel and Paddington Packet Boat, while the Cowley Brick was more distant, but a reminder of that lost industry. The General Elliott and Dolphin remain in the middle of Uxbridge, both on the water, the first of these is where I would get to know some of those from the early punk bands that came from the area, namely Leigh Heggarty of The Price and now Ruts DC, Manic Esso from The Lurkers, and Paul Fox of The Ruts.

Paul lived on a narrowboat moored thirty seconds from the back of the pub, and this was in the early years of the current century, not long after my novel *Human Punk* was published, a story that draws on the Slough Arm, and while drinking with these men, members of bands I had seen as a teenager but who I now knew as friends, it felt as if fiction and fact were merging. Again, I suppose this was true, as an author's memories and influences are always in the mix, a major part of the writing process.

Human Punk tells the story of a teenager from Slough called Joe Martin, and how an incident that takes place in the summer of 1977 changes his life. Walking home late one night, Joe and his best friend Smiles are stopped as they cross the canal, attacked by four youths who object to the Sex Pistols badge Smiles is wearing. They are beaten up and thrown off the bridge and into the water below, with Smiles becoming entangled in the weeds and rubbish, stuck below the surface for too long. He is pulled out and saved, but, more so than Joe, is never the same. Towards the end of the novel, set in 2000, Joe returns to the canal and lowers himself into water, reliving that earlier experience. The past and the present combine, memory giving way to renewal, which is maybe how I see the canals today.

The waterways are cleaner and busier that I remember, and while this is obviously a good thing, I can't help feeling nostalgic for that post-war decay, even though the canals remain special, and the locks keep amazing. These days, living elsewhere, I walk further afield, out from Brentford to Hanwell and on to Southall, or along the Regent's Canal where a friend lives on a narrowboat, moving between Willesden and Kings Cross. While it is easy to romanticise the slower-paced, shabby peace of the past, it is just as easy to ignore the realities of those serving the Industrial Revolution. It would have been a hard enough for the humans grafting on the canals, but not as hard as it was for the horses forced to slave on its towpaths. Some would have been treated better than others, but all were brutalised to differing degrees, their reward a trip to the horrors of the slaughterhouse.

Earlier this year I added to the *Satellite Cycle* that started with *Human Punk* and continued with *White Trash* and

Skinheads, releasing the novel *London Country*, and while I drew on the canal briefly, and especially the White Bridge and its Denham setting, it is in my new novella *Grand Union* where it takes centre stage.

Grand Union is one third of *The View From Poacher's Hill*, which includes stories by Irvine Welsh and Alan Warner, and is a second collection following on from *The Seal Club*, published in 2020. My contribution to that was *The Beasts Of Brussels*, and one of its passing characters is Merlin, a lorry driver from Birmingham who has bought himself a narrowboat and dreams of one day leaving the pressures of motorway and long-distance European driving behind to travel around England on the older paths. He considers how life has speeded up, the shift from barges to the railways to lorries, the change in the sort of horsepower employed.

While it wasn't planned at the time, Merlin in turn led to *Grand Union*, which places him firmly in the spotlight. Struggling to find work as the first Covid lockdown comes into effect, and already sick of the wages and conditions, the way lorry drivers are treated, he realises he has to change his life, that if he doesn't swim he will sink. Used to being on the move, he can't bear to be stuck indoors, decides to bring his plans forward and live his dream. He leaves his flat and dumps his belongings with his brother, collects his goat Gary and sets off on *Wizard's Journey* to explore England. It is an adventure for both man and beast, and while there are challenges, some temper tantrums and even headbutting from the goat, in time they settle into a routine where understanding and a mutual respect rules.

Merlin has come to terms with the quiet and defeated his early loneliness, learning how to move and maintain *Wizard's Journey*, aims to travel every mile of the canals, to pass through every lock and cross every viaduct. He has thought about the horses of the past and dealt with his fear that the towpath is haunted by their spirits, knows now that the clacking of hooves belongs to the goat. Moving unseen through the back channels, Merlin and Gary are in fine form as they moor outside Rickmansworth and prepare to enter Uxbridge in the morning. His football pals from the England scene are meeting up in a canalside pub, drawn by a combination of Merlin himself, Gary Goat and their means of transport. A large crowd is anticipated, a union of diverse characters about to take place, although there are of course problems to be resolved.

Maybe the parts of the system I know aren't the most beautiful or dramatic, and for seasoned travellers only ever passed through, but they are personal to me, belong to a mental as well as physical landscape. Time slows and I see the past, particularly my childhood and youth, yet the Grand Union around Uxbridge and the Slough Arm also feel somehow timeless. They carry submerged memories and imaginings, facts and fictions, and it has surprised me how these keep bubbling up out of my subconscious, suggesting new stories to tell. I hope this continues for a good while yet.

A Very Corporate Coup

Despite the denials of our political and media classes, the most important issue at this year's election is Britain's membership of the European Union. It undermines the major debates and warps most of the policies being put forward. The EU will influence the future of the NHS just as it helped smooth Tory privatisation of the Post Office and the organisational break-up of the railways; it is in tune with Coalition austerity and drives a larger and more deadly version in the eurozone; it escalates problems linked to housing, work, wages and education; creates worry and stirs up anger and threatens people's sense of identity. A casual acceptance of establishment propaganda and a fear of being branded 'xenophobic' has silenced many liberals and left-wingers, and yet the EU is driven by big business. This is a very corporate coup.

It is essential to understand where the European Union is heading. The mission? To create a centralised superstate. As former Commission president Jose Manuel Barroso said in 2007: 'I like to compare the EU as a creation to the organisation of empire. We have the dimension of empire.' While there have been idealists involved and progressive laws made along the way, at its core it is undemocratic and distant and right-wing, a threat to all those living in its shadow. However sweet the propaganda, it a tool for the multinationals, another part of the globalisation process.

A majority of the British population are either opposed to or sceptical of our inclusion in the European Union and yet any serious discussion of what it represents and where it is leading is near enough impossible. Instead we have McCarthy-like campaigns directed at those who have a different vision for Britain and the other member countries. And yet decades of that pro-EU spin have failed to convince the mass of working people of its worth, the only reason their opposition is so restrained is the secrecy and speed of the takeover. This has occurred across generations, a slow-motion transfer of control driven by the rich and powerful. Our leaders are complicit, know where their futures rest. There are careers to protect and promote, fortunes to be made. The feelings of the wider society are ignored.

The idea put across by its promoters, that the EU is somehow synonymous with 'Europe', is nonsense, and yet this use of language has become commonplace in certain circles. We are told that to be anti-EU is to be 'anti-European', but in reality, to oppose the EU makes you *pro*-European. If Europe is its people and cultures, then surely it is better that France, Greece, Poland and every other member state becomes a real democracy again. If the main legacy of the European Enlightenment was the collectivisation of political power in the hands of the masses, then the EU model is the antithesis of this, centralising decision-taking in the hands of an unaccountable technocratic elite.

Difference is healthy. The continent doesn't have to be homogenised and repackaged by the Brussels machine. The so-called Metric Martyrs were laughed at for standing up to this obsession with conformity, while the fact that a rare vote on EU policy by a member state is often held a second time if a 'no' result is reached is considered amusing by some. But this is serious stuff. It reeks of a dictatorship, albeit a subtle one.

A single European nation suits the US government, its multinationals and military. One leader is a lot easier to deal with than many. The same goes for a single currency. This is clear in moves by the EU and the US to impose the Transatlantic Trade And Investment Partnership (TTIP), which will allow the corporations of both blocks the chance to exploit each other's markets, smoothing out 'obstacles' in the process. The NHS would be targeted by US healthcare companies and trade-union rights threatened. Negotiations to bring in TTIP have been taking place in secret. There is no voting involved, no pretence at democracy, little proper coverage by the media. The main parties are broadly supportive. With TTIP comes Investor-State Dispute Settlements, whereby business can take governments to court if their profits are infringed upon. This is mind-blowing stuff, needs to be confronted head on during this election, but instead our politicians hide, happy to talk and talk but scared to say anything. Confusion is allowed to reign.

The media tells us that the Tories are anti-EU while Labour and the Lib-Dems are fighting their narrow-mindedness, UKIP dismissed as a far-right group bordering on the fascist. This is bubblegum politics. Little Europeans sneer 'Little Englander' at those with a different opinion, pedalling stereotypes, unwilling to consider the bigger arguments.

The fact that it was the Conservatives which took Britain into a six-nation Common Market in 1973 is dismissed. This was a betrayal of the Commonwealth, which a mere twenty-eight years earlier had fought with us against two of these countries, the then fascist Germany and Italy. Commonwealth economies suffered as a result. Prime minister Ted Heath insisted the Common Market was no more than a trade arrangement, but a large chunk of the population was outraged, saw it for what it was, and Heath would later admit he had lied about its long-term goal. Labour was socialist at this point and along with the trade unions naturally opposed the Tories. Despite some big talk, Margaret Thatcher and John Major did not take us out, while Little Tory Blair would have stuck the UK in the eurozone if he'd had his way.

David Cameron is pro-EU but has been forced towards a referendum by rebel elements within his party, while Ed Miliband is also a supporter, his own sceptical backbenchers may be quiet for fear of being branded right-wing by the party's thought police. Backing the European Union just because the Tories are supposedly against it is pretty pathetic. The EU is not a party issue, as has been shown by UKIP establishing itself as the main challenger to Labour in many northern constituencies. It is much more important.

Last year saw the death of two genuinely left-wing figures within a matter of days in Tony Benn and Bob Crow. These were honest men who refused to bend to the group mind. They were idealists and knew where the EU is leading. Both were attacked by Labour figures as well as the Tories, in later life Benn was patronised as a well-meaning crank when he tried to talk seriously about the EU. Crow died young and his dream of a left-wing anti-EU party will be harder to achieve now that he is gone. But this is what Britain needs. Urgently.

The move towards a European state is a long way down the line and yet even this simple truth is denied by those whose careers are sewn into the process. Talk of changing an EU policy here, pushing for a reform there, is meaningless when the long-term mission is to create a new empire. The only answer is to withdraw. Instead our controllers look forward to a well-paid semi-retirement in Brussels. The EU's friends are very well treated. It doesn't matter if it is Leon Brittan, Neil Kinnock or Blair, our politicians quickly merge into one.

As things stand, the EU makes a large percentage of our laws and its judges can overrule our courts. According to House Of Commons library research, if regulations as well as directives are counted, half of UK laws are derived from Brussels, measures that cannot be reversed once passed, but if even one law is made outside Parliament then that is a huge abuse of power. And yet this has been going on for years. The EU has a president, a militarised police force in EUROGENDFOR, is pushing for its own army, has helped stir up the crisis in the Ukraine with its expansionism. Its single currency has caused untold misery for tens of millions of working people across Europe, but there is no apology, just an arrogant demand for greater powers. The EU talks instead about 'liberalisation'. This is classic doublespeak, a Brussels speciality. Spain, Italy, Ireland know the reality. The Greeks are branded lazy and forced to cut services in return for more loans. Along with the Italians they have seen EU technocrats imposed on their government.

If there is a referendum on our EU membership in the next Parliament, the propaganda unleashed by the establishment will be unparalleled. From *The Guardian* to the *Times*, from the BBC to Murdoch, our masters will close ranks as withdrawal is deemed a disaster. But would Britain be damaged? For a start we would save around £10 billion a year in our net handout to the EU. This is a massive sum, which if used properly would benefit those who actually pay these siphoned-off taxes. The idea that our neighbours would no longer trade with us is simply untrue. Trade would continue and we would be able to deal with the rest of the world more freely. Only about fifteen percent of British GDP is accounted for by our exports to the rest of the EU and this percentage is falling as the eurozone stagnates. The future for Britain lies with building ever better trade relations with the economically expanding parts of the world, such as the Commonwealth countries. Britain would be liberated.

Most of the arguments against EU membership are left-leaning and liberal. UKIP has done well because it largely tells the truth about the EU, even if some of its tactics and emphasis put people off. The fact that it can pull in Labour voters despite its Thatcherite, non-patriotic economics and some bongoland backers should be revealing. This has to tell Labour something, surely? But no... Just as depressing has been the cowardice of the so-called independent parties. The Greens, SNP and Plaid Cymru exist to promote localism and the devolution of power, yet they refuse to challenge an EU which is about the *centralising* of power, a closed organisation that dwarfs the actions of the 'Westminster' elite they criticise but in this instance mimic. It makes no sense unless they are either a smaller part of the same establishment or blinded by their hatred of the Tories.

The Scottish Referendum quickly became about money rather than identity, yet nobody talked about the madness of a standalone Scotland re-entering the EU as a new applicant and adopting the euro. Why would the SNP want to gain independence and then hand it over to a larger, more remote body, where it would have less say than now in how it runs its own affairs? Why would it want to have even less control of its economy? You only have to look at Sinn Fein's attempts to keep Ireland out of the euro for a comparison. The whole debate on Scotland leaving the UK was pretty pointless if the SNP's willingness to join the EU wasn't challenged. If the SNP wanted its own currency and with that a truly independent nation it would have made sense, but leave the UK and join the EU instead?

When it comes to worries over immigration the Right and Left are useless. Take away the kneejerk reactions on both sides and it is largely about numbers and the resulting threat to jobs and wages, the pressure on housing, healthcare and education. Is it wrong to want jobs to go to local people? Neither should foreigners be used as scapegoats for the failures of our politicians. Most people are pretty fair about all this, but if a job can be filled by a local then that is seen as right. This protects community, should be applied regionally as well. But the focus on immigration is a smokescreen, suits the major parties as it shifts attention from the important questions that need to be confronted about our EU membership.

It is a simple fact that nothing can be done to control the numbers coming in from the EU as long as we are a member, but why would only two of the seven political leaders admit this in a recent TV debate? This sort of deceit drives people mad. Open borders are essential to the EU's single state. It makes for a more mobile (often cheaper) workforce on one level, allows business and the wealthy easy access on another. It will also change voting patterns, as there will come a point when elections are going to be open to whoever lives in a country at a given time. There has always been movement of people and there always will be. Leaving the EU will not stop this, just take us away from the Fortress Europe model.

UKIP targets poorer workers, highlighting the threat to working-class jobs and wages in the same way certain trade unions do, but it ignores 'high-end' immigration and the negative effect this has had on the lives of the everyday person, especially in and around London. Everything we have is up for sale and the rich and powerful of the world are making a fortune at our expense. House prices are driven up and new properties sold as investments rather than homes. Large areas of London have seen local people driven out, their culture erased. This creates huge ripples than spread through the rest of the country. It is natural to feel angry at this unfairness.

We are continually told that Britain's muted opposition to the EU is somehow a quirk that shows us to be intolerant, but we are one of the most open-minded countries in the world. And the idea that every European is happy being in the EU is untrue. Most are resigned, feel more powerless and despondent than we do. The need for a left-wing opposition to the EU should be taken care of by the Labour Party, but it lost its nerve when Thatcher was in power, along with elements in the trade-union movement selling its soul to Brussels in return for some positive legislation. Then it was hijacked and turned into New Labour. It has yet to recover.

Most important in all this is people's sense of identity. This is rarely mentioned by anyone with a public voice, maybe for fear of being branded 'racist'. The less you have, maybe the more your identity matters, and a powerful elite do not have the right to sell this off to the EU or anyone else. Our controllers, tucked away in their big houses, worshipping money either openly or from behind their fake-liberal lectures, do not understand or care about this, and yet it is in the mass population where the real integration has always occurred, where diversity isn't measured by the colour of your skin. This is ongoing, part of the British tradition. It is no shame to want to preserve your culture.

During the election campaign Tony Blair argued that the people should not be given the chance to vote in an EU referendum as we could not be trusted to make the 'sensible choice'. His elitist questioning of the intelligence of the electorate is no different to those nineteenth-century reactionary Tories who argued on similar grounds that the franchise should not be extended to women and members of the working class. Most within our political and media classes and big business seem to think the same way as Blair, want the EU issue sidelined, ruled off limits for democratic debate.

The EU offers us little. It costs billions to belong to a club that interferes in our affairs and has created needless divisions, one that will ultimately lead to our removal from the map. If a European superstate is achieved, the resentment and anger will flow through the centuries to come, creating resistance movements right across the continent. Leaving the EU would save us money which could (in the right hands) be ploughed back into the public sector to safeguard jobs and services. And yet nearly every mainstream politician lifts their nose in the air and turns away, embarrassed at ideas they consider crass. Across the world people are fighting to be more independent, not less. They crave democracy and accountability, want to see their identities and cultures live on. The EU is not new and it is not progressive, its trail winding back to the Roman Empire. Britain needs to look to the future.

The Shed

I WAS STANDING OUTSIDE Stamford Bridge with my father, in the crush of people trying to get into the ground, when 'Liquidator' by Harry J All Stars started playing on the PA system, the skinhead classic suddenly joined by the thunder of rhythmic clapping and the roar of 'England'. The year was 1970. Chelsea were at home to Southampton and I was nine years old. My skin tingled then and it tingles now, remembering the moment when I realised football is about much more than twenty-two men kicking a round object up and down a patch of grass.

The sound came from under what looked like an old metal roof at the top of a big concrete wall on the other side of the turnstiles, but before we could get inside these were closed and we ended up on the small terrace in front of the East Stand. This was my first game and the players seemed to have halos around them as they ran onto the pitch, but while I was excited to see my heroes in real life I kept looking at the terrace to my left. It was packed. Especially under the roof at the back. The crowd in there was singing and chanting, surging up and down. I could see a lot of policemen. Something was going on. This was The Shed. This was where I wanted to be.

My next two games again saw The Shed full early and the turnstiles closed, for the visits of Manchester United and Tottenham. On both occasions, we ended up on the terrace at the opposite end of the ground, which gave me another view of The Shed, which seemed even bigger and more impressive than before. The away end had a spooky little stand that looked like something from Alfred Hitchcock's *Psycho*. Built in the late-1930s, it was meant to run along the back of the entire terrace, but work was interrupted by the war and never completed, and that has been my experience of Stamford Bridge over the decades, a stadium that evolves in stops and starts, much like the club before its current run of success.

When I finally made it into The Shed we stood towards the front and at the side, where it was easier for a child to see the pitch. I think it was a 4–0 win over Everton, but could be wrong. That game sticks in in my head for the two goals Peter Osgood scored, but more so for the glow created by the flood-lights, how they illuminated the yellow shirts of the Everton players. Floodlit football was always a joy at Stamford Bridge, the fact that the stands were set back from the pitch intensifying the effect. It was the same at Wembley.

Chelsea had recently won the FA Cup, adding silverware to their flamboyance. This was the era of the so-called maverick, flair players considered too individualistic for the national side. While a team was lucky to have one such player – George Best at Manchester United and Rodney Marsh at QPR, for instance – at Chelsea we had three in Osgood, Alan Hudson and Charlie Cooke. They were part of a group of players famed for their drinking, and the fact Stamford Bridge is situated near the Kings Road meant they were perfectly located to enjoy the pubs and nightclubs of the Swinging Sixties and early Seventies. Chelsea were seen as a rebel club, the players hard to control, and the supporters followed their example. With a big young support mainly coming out of West London, South London and the suburbs and new towns beyond, The Shed had a reputation. It was considered one of the great terraces along with The Kop at Liverpool and The Stretford End at Manchester United.

The Sixties had seen visiting supporters going into home ends looking for a fight, the idea being to chase the opposition out and take the end. Skinheads were synonymous with this aggro, and Chelsea boasted big numbers. This taking of ends was happening less in the 1970s, or at least at Chelsea, where the visitors stood little chance of success. West Ham and Millwall were the only ones I remember coming in during this time. The skinhead look had mutated into a scruffier boot-boy appearance, and the Seventies were the heyday of our terrace culture. Chart-based bands such as Slade and Sweet were popular, while the greatest terrace single remains 'Saturday Night's Alright For Fighting' by Watford FC's pub-piano player Elton John.

Like most football grounds – and post-war Britain generally – Stamford Bridge was rundown and crumbling. Originally an athletics stadium, the stands were set back from the pitch to allow for a running track, which was unusual and gave the stadium a Continental feel. This track was later used for greyhound racing and speedway, the roof at the back of the home end added to shelter bookmakers from the rain. It looked like a shed and it was christened The Shed, Cliff Webb credited with the renaming of the Fulham Road End after his letter appeared in a match-day programme in 1966. Along with the likes of Mick Greenaway and Danny Eccles, the Webb brothers were vital in the forming of The Shed End, the creation of a vocal home support.

As I got older I wanted to go to football with my friends and stand further into The Shed, and my match-day experience changed. The potential for trouble was a big attraction for my generation of kids, it can't be denied, but what I remember most is the singing and humour, an incredible sense of belonging. It became part of our identity. We *were* Chelsea. We *were* The Shed. As one chorus put it: 'We are the boys who make the most noise, we are the Chelsea – boot boys…'

Popular records and folk songs were adapted, the Cockney favourite 'Knees Up Mother Brown' done straight, a knees-up that spilled down the terrace, while 'My Old Man (Said Follow The Van)' was changed into a song that rolled off the tongue: 'My old man, said be a Chelsea fan, and don't dilly dally on the way, we'll take the Tottenham in half a minute, we'll take the North Bank and all that's in it, with hatchets and hammers, carving knives and spanners, we'll show those Tottenham bastards how to fight… 'Not that I saw any weapons. It was just a song. Using a knife was seen as effeminate, cowardly, unBritish.

Gary Glitter's 'Hello, Hello, I'm Back Again' became the more relevant and urgent chant 'Hello, Hello, Chelsea Aggro, Chelsea Aggro, Hello…' while another short sharp favourite was 'You're going to get your fucking heads kicked in'. Most of the songs related to fighting, and it was important to include the word 'fuck'. So The Shed had its share of lyricists, terrace poets who must have spent a lot of time searching for the best rhymes. Different people stood in different areas, largely according to age and inclination. If you supported Chelsea, you were welcome.

Following the 1970 FA Cup win, the club planned to rebuild Stamford Bridge as a futuristic super-stadium. The East Stand was knocked down and replaced with a structure that remains impressive to this day, but the collapse of the economy and mounting debts saw Chelsea go into decline and the work stopped. The mavericks left, there was little money for new players, and the crowds fell. The Shed remained loyal, and travelled away in impressive numbers, even when Chelsea were relegated to the Second Division, and a few years later, on the verge of dipping into the Third.

Some of the worst times on the pitch were some of the best times off it, with the core support remaining loyal. There were games when the attendance was dire, in tune with the terrible football, but this was when the humour shone through. The football itself didn't matter now. Other games saw the ground packed with the incredible atmosphere of the past returning, especially when we played someone like Liverpool or Tottenham in the FA Cup.

My first full season in The Shed was 1976–77, coinciding with the arrival of punk, the Sex Pistols forming on the Kings Road. By this time, Chelsea were festering in the Second Division, but a young side emerged under manager Eddie McCreadie, a much loved former player. The club was broke and on its knees, but Eddie Mac built a side in which all but one player had come through the youth system. Led by Ray Wilkins, this was the supporters' team, and that season has to be my favourite ever. The Shed was packed for every game and the crush was so great I would take my feet off the floor and see how long I could be carried along. Chelsea were promoted and returned to the First Division in style. It can honestly be said that that Chelsea side was made in The Shed.

Sadly, the money problems remained, Eddie McCreadie left, and Chelsea were relegated again, not returning to the top flight until 1984. Ken Bates bought the club for £1 and took on its debts, but didn't get the leasehold, a battle following as developers wanted to kick the club out and build on the land. A property crash meant the situation was resolved, and once he had the freehold Bates did something very special. He created the Chelsea Pitch Owners (CPO), a non-profit company owned by the supporters who bought (and can buy) a £100 share to become a member. The pitch (and name) thereby belongs to the fans. This is unique in the Premier League.

The years passed, full of ups and lots of downs, but the excitement of going to games, even if it had become more of a need, was a big part of our social lives. Walking down the Fulham Road, through the turnstiles, up the steps to The Shed... Drinking was an important part of the culture and the area around the ground was blessed with plenty of decent pubs in those days. In 1992 the Premier League was formed, and two years later The Shed saw its last game, a 3–2 win against Sheffield United. It was a sad, depressing day. Some people went to the pub to toast the memories, more of us just went home. Shortly after The Shed was turned to rubble.

All-seater stadia were being introduced, and while the authorities said it was to make things safer for the spectators, we knew it was really a way of gentrifying the game for the business interests who smelled satellite-TV money and wanted a share. There has been lots of great football played at Stamford Bridge since, and Chelsea have achieved fantastic things on the pitch, but that terrace culture we loved will never return to the ground. It lives on, of course, but is more than ever separated from the club. It is the same across the Premier League, part of the globalisation process, where localism and a genuine loyalty that goes beyond the money-motive has to be removed.

The oldest part of the ground now is the East Stand, built in the early 1970s. Next is the Matthew Harding Stand, which replaced the North Stand, built thanks to lifelong Chelsea supporter Matthew, tragically killed in a helicopter crash in 1996. The dog track is gone and the stands are close to the pitch. The facilities have massively improved, which is a good thing, but the decades of lecturing on what we can and can't do and say and think has taken its toll. Even so, lots of people raised in The Shed are still attending games, and the support remains defiant and proud.

Chelsea are one of only three Premiership clubs still playing at their original ground. There has been talk of a new stadium on the current site, while ten years ago the club wanted to move to a different location. This was opposed by the CPO members. At a meeting in 2011, The Shed stepped out of the shadows and the club's proposal to acquire the leasehold in order to sell the land and facilitate the move was voted down. This was despite attempts to achieve a Yes vote with the late buying of blocks of shares. The fury of the supporters forced the club to shelve their plans, but the trust has yet to mend.

While Stamford Bridge is sterile compared to the place I first went to as a child, the piecemeal nature of the improvements have left it with a character other brand-new stadia lack. The football has been spectacular and few of us can complain about what has been achieved. Mick Greenaway is no longer be with us, but his famous 'Zigger Zagger' chant can still be heard, while 'Liquidator' is played before and after each game. The crowd claps and sings along, and my skin tingles.

May Day

Britain is in turmoil – the people are fed up with the excesses of big business; workers are told to increase production for less pay; the wealthy meet to plan how they can become even richer; the unions try to mobilise the power of the masses; links between government, arms-manufacturers and the media are hinted at but never proven; disillusionment spreads; a march takes place; the police clash with demonstrators; a man is killed on the streets of London. This could be Britain today, but it is also a summary of some of the events driving *May Day* – a novel by John Sommerfield, first published in 1936.

Set over three days, sometime during the 1930s, a snappy, italicised description of London sets the scene – '*The sky oozes soot and aeroplanes, and burns by night with an electric glow. Railways writhe like worms under the clay, tangled with spiderwebs and mazes of electric cables, drains and gaspipes. Then there are the eight or nine million people.*' *May Day* is about these people – their hopes, successes, mistakes, regrets, dreams, reality. Slogans show the way ahead – ALL OUT ON MAY DAY... WORKERS OF THE WORLD UNITE. The busmen are going to strike and everyone is talking about their union's plans for May 1st – the day of the workers. Change is in the air.

John Sommerfield was a politically active man who rejected the bullying aspects of capitalism and, for a period of his life, was an active member of the Communist Party. He marched and spoke at meetings and had his front teeth knocked out in a fight with either the police or fascists. He fought in one of the International Brigades during the Spanish Civil War and, like many idealists at this time, held firm views on how society needed to improve. He was also open-minded, a lifelong optimist, someone who believed in the worth of each individual, and it is these qualities that elevate *May Day* above much of the fiction dealing in social struggle.

This belief in the individual shows itself in the large number of characters who make up *May Day*. No single voice dominates, no central character is in control. The political is made very personal as a series of smaller sketches connect to form the bigger picture. Scenes shift and faces change, but the links are neat and effective – some complementary, others adding contrast and conflict – and they always push the novel forward. It is a complex, experimental approach, which could easily have failed, losing direction and focus, but Sommerfield pulls it off. The result is a fluent, highly-imaginative piece of writing.

The author's own experiences, as well as his beliefs, back up the text. The first of the larger characters to appear is James Seton – communist, seaman, Civil War veteran; like Sommerfield – who is on a ship anchored off Gravesend, waiting to return to London. The next scene shows his brother John and Martine, their child and dog, sleeping in a humble house near the Harrow Road. John is a carpenter at Langfier's Carbon Works, and while aware that trouble is brewing, he has been unemployed so Martine doesn't want him to strike, fearing he will lose his job. (Sommerfield had also worked as a carpenter and spent periods unemployed.)

The first day dawns and the Thames is heaving with ships, the great dockyards of East London throbbing with activity, and soon we are inside the Carbon Works where 'two hundred and forty girls in ugly grey overalls and caps live, breathe and think, their fragile flesh confused with the greasy embraces of steel tentacles.' They are on piecework rather than proper pay, and the bosses are demanding a 'speed-up'. These young women are kept on until they are twenty-one and then let go, as their rate would have to be increased. The conditions are cramped and dangerous, and the girls are tired. Machines roar and hands are mangled. This is the world of Daisy Miller, Molly Davis and Ivy Cutford. The London Match-Girls Strike of 1888 hovers in the background.

From Langfier's Carbon Works the book spirals off into the wider city, dipping in and out of the lives of the Seton brothers and the bosses and a wide selection of connecting men and women, spreading out from East London into the West End and West London, crossing boundaries of sex and class, moving from terraced streets and factories to detached villas and parks. The book starts to build towards May Day.

Generally in literature, and the arts in general, then as now, the common people are stereotyped or belittled, or if they are lucky treated as curiosities before being dismissed to the margins, so when a novel is written from a more sympathetic position it is natural for the author to want to reverse the prejudice – but John Sommerfield resists this temptation. He remains even-handed and rejects a more dogmatic approach, and by doing so opens the story right up, showing that maybe the bosses aren't benefitting as much as their power and wealth would suggest.

The best example of this is Sir Edwin Langfier, owner of the Carbon Works, who comes across as a decent man, but someone whose real power has been lost in a deal with Amalgamated Industrial Enterprises, a big organisation with a cynical approach to business. We see him in his chauffeur-driven Daimler, passing through Hyde Park, reaching Commercial Road, travelling along East India Dock Road, heading towards the shipyards, a rich man in one of the greatest cities on the planet, yet despite his position in society he is disillusioned and empty inside. His wife is the same, while their son Peter lacks any meaning to his life – walking in the park, attending a society dance, searching for love. Everyone is looking for love, whatever their backgrounds, but it is John and Martine who are happiest together – making do, Martine shopping in Portobello Road market while John grafts at the factory, appreciating what they have because it has been earned.

Towards the end of the book Sir Edwin tells Peter that he has let his son down, that because he has never had to work for anything he lacks direction. Against the odds, the reader feels sadness for the Langfier family, and by achieving this reaction Sommerfield strengthens the novel and shows that, on a deeper and more meaningful level, an exploitative system is no good for anyone – rich or poor.

Family connections are clearly important, a concentration of the larger family perhaps – John and James Seton; the powerful (and well-named) Sloane brothers; Sir Edwin and his son Peter. James is a loner in many ways, married to his politics, searching for his brother, but he doesn't find him until late in the novel, and not in the sort of circumstances either would have wanted. By chance James meets an old friend, Pat Morgan, and this other sort of brother is an interesting addition.

A sub-editor on a leading newspaper, Morgan is a communist and former comrade of James Seton, from either seafaring days or the Spanish Civil War. Pat's workmate is Vernon – the name of John Sommerfield's father... a journalist – and through their work Morgan sees what the newspaper's owner is planning to write about the busmen and their May Day protest. He visits one of the printers, Jackson, an older communist. We are left with impressions... possibilities.

When tragedy hits the Carbon Works, Ivy Cutford steps forward and finds her voice, mobilising the other girls in a doubly brave move given the position of working women at the time. Some of the most downtrodden members of the workforce stand up and fight back. The May Day march is passing... the factory gates are locked... mounted police fight the marchers... a truncheon is raised in the air. It is one of the most symbolic and dramatic passages in the book. The great propaganda posters of the period are unfurled in the reader's mind.

Writing nearly fifty years after the book was first published, in May 1984, in his *Note* to a new edition, Sommerfield said: 'When I wrote it I'd have probably said that *May Day* was socialist realism. Now I'd call it early '30s communist romanticism. I'm not in any way apologising for the book's enthusiastic, simple-minded political idealism. Because it was a genuine idealism.'

He is being modest. There is plenty of social realism in *May Day*, and while there is also simple-minded idealism, that has to be better than cynicism – or apathy. His optimism is clear throughout the novel, but also in the *Note*, which is reproduced at the back of this London Books edition. He romanticises communism, but this wasn't unusual in the 1930s. Being a British communist in 1936 was very different to being one in 1984, when the gulags and terrors were well-documented. This was the time of the Miner's Strike, when the term was casually used to smear anyone who believed in worker's rights and the importance of a trade union.

Sommerfield also writes about the changes that had occurred in Britain since *May Day* was written, the better living conditions enjoyed by working people, and that only 'the truly rich and powerful' carried on regardless, as if nothing had changed except for 'electronic improvements in the means of selling goods and bending minds'. Twenty-six years since he wrote those words, and seventy-four years after *May Day* first appeared, the rich and powerful are still doing what they want, while the internet and digital technology mean the selling and bending have gone into overdrive.

Following his death in 1991, another wave of change has swamped us. The exploiters are the same, but come in different masks to 1984, never mind 1936. Cool Britannia, the For Sale sticker stuck to every element of our infrastructure and culture, privatisation and globalisation and the expansion of the EU superstate, free-enterprise crusades and a nation in debt to mobile-phone companies, ultra-surveillance and a tightening of state control, the ever-increasing slaughter of the meat and dairy industries, a loss of national law-making and boundaries, the digital breakdown of life into dots on a computer screen, multinational threats to copyright laws – maybe even novels themselves.

Idealistic literature, whether naive or not, is more important than ever. Rather than a cut-price file to decorate yet another appliance, it can offer an honest and independent take on life that is beyond money. It stimulates free-thought, promotes imagination, invites people to create their own imagery and stretch their minds rather than have them bent by big business. Books such as *May Day* matter. Conditions have obviously improved massively since it was written, but they did so because there were idealist men and women willing to fight for change. Those who want to control and exploit others are still with us and will never go away, it is just their methods that have changed. Books from the past tell us about our lives today. Everything changes... nothing changes.

The 1930s produced a rich seam of London authors who captured the grittier side of society in their fiction – James Curtis, Gerald Kersh and Robert Westerby are some of the best – and John Sommerfield belongs in this company. He was a regular in The Fitzroy Tavern, just north of Soho, and knew at least Curtis and Kersh, who also drank there, along with the likes of George Orwell, Julian Maclaren-Ross and Dylan Thomas.

The so-called 'lowlife' novels of Curtis, Kersh and Westerby – *The Gilt Kid*, *Night And The City* and *Wide Boys*

Never Work being examples – are set in the criminal alleyways of London life, and in particular the broader Soho area. This was an exotic location that drifted into theatreland and the older areas of exoticism and sleaze around Piccadilly and the Strand. The West End was a world away from the factories and dockyards of East London, a place where classes and nationalities mixed, the daily grind of industrial labour remote and ignored, and yet the lives of the prostitutes and villains who fill these books were rooted in these communities.

Curtis, a dedicated socialist, a more 'difficult' man than Sommerfield, but someone who lived and suffered for his principles, was interested in language, and his work captures the speech and slang of a range of working-class characters in a unique and vital way. Yet Curtis was also concerned with prejudice, and in particular the unfairness of the judicial system. He deals with miscarriages of justice, with the threat and reality of capital punishment. Interestingly, the hangman Pierrepoint was another regular in the Fitzroy Tavern. So too was Robert Fabian, aka Fabian Of The Yard.

In *Night And The City*, Kersh positions Harry Fabian – a cockney ponce and chancer, who tries to sell his girlfriend into slavery – against his honest, costermonger brother Bert. Fabian attempts to pass himself off as an American, mimicking the movies, but despite his charisma he is a desperate man doomed to failure. *Wide Boys Never Work*, meanwhile, sees Jim Bankley leave his job in a car factory and travel to London after witnessing a Soho razor-gang in action at his local racecourse. He is impressed by their flash motors and sharp suits, and ends up joining the Franks mob, his hard-working father performing the same role as Bert. In these books the main characters are trying to escape the hard labour of their backgrounds through crime. They are dreamers.

In *May Day*, John Sommerfield has attempted something very different. His working-class heroes are interested in self-improvement, the struggle against exploitation, and in some cases the removal of capitalism itself. This is the common people in their more everyday form. *May Day* deals in labourers and craftsmen and factory girls who would never dream of turning to prostitution – though Sommerfield does create the character Jenny Hardy to show the choices some women make, in this case one driven by want rather than need. AIE man Dartry has set up Jenny – a former Carbon Works girl – as his mistress. She has a flat in a nice part of London, with cash and jewellery and a secret boyfriend she hides from Dartry. She has rejected the factory floor, and in Jenny we see a clear recognition of the truths written about by Curtis, Kersh and Westerby.

The majority of Sommerfield's working-class characters are keen to take on their enemies rather than imitate their values. On the surface this might not seem as exciting as the 'lowlife' approach, but Sommerfield is a fine author whose writing overflows with energy and empathy. *May Day*, and a similar novel from the period, Simon Blumenfeld's excellent *Jew Boy*, complement *The Gilt Kid*, *Night And The City* and *Wide Boys Never Work*. Together they present a broad picture of working-class London in the pre-War years, and a reflection of the society in which we live today.

On its publication, *Left Review* called *May Day* 'the best collective novel that we have yet produced in England', and the prose never weakens. The text is loaded with philosophy and observation, glimpses of more and more lives, the endless tangle of those 'eight or nine million people' – the Langfier's maid Jean visits her grandfather in hospital... he has been moved from the workhouse and is dying of consumption... a surgeon operates to save the life of Mrs Riley... while her son Bolshi Bill fights for a fairer society... but the leader of the largest trade-union is enjoying his power and wealth and craves arbitration... and all the time nature pushes at the bricks and mortar of the city... the trees blossom... spring scents the air.... May arrives... a baby is born... nearby there is loneliness and fear... another mother kills her unwanted child... and a great yearning for love and meaning presses at the minds of the people. *Left Review* rightly added: 'Sommerfield gives us the true London – smelt, seen, understood.'

The book culminates in the May Day march, the clash of controllers and controlled, the people heading towards Marble Arch where General Fitzroy struts, passing along Fleet Street on the way, watched by Pat Morgan, a free spirit lurking inside the pre-Wapping machine. The General Strike of 1926 is referred to often, as something to recall with pride, to emulate, a lesson from history. The message is clear – the struggle continues. The last line of *May Day* reads: 'Everyone has agreed on the need for a big change.' Again, those words could have been written today.

"Call Me Elvis"

John King Interviewed By Allan Kausch

So vegan for many years, but not straightedge?

I like drinking. In pubs. With friends. For me, being vegan is all about the cruelty involved in meat and dairy. Knowing what is done to those creatures on the receiving end makes me sick. There are no good reasons for the slaughter. Not in today's refrigerated world. That has to be a core value, and it is bizarre seeing people dressed in leather lecturing others about their politics. Sitting there with rotting flesh in their systems as they pontificate about minutiae. I have never thought about it in terms of health, although I agree that a vegan diet is going to be better. That wasn't something that came into it as much when I became vegetarian in the early 1980s, or vegan in the early 1990s.

I admire those who are straightedge, though, their strength of mind, but pubs are a big part of my culture. There are few things better than a proper session, just sitting there drinking and talking in a traditional old boozer. It is good for the mental health. *My* mental health. Beer washes the worries away. Rinses my brain. This is purely social, as I rarely drink at home and never alone. Thinking about it, apart from stout and coffee, I suppose I'm not that far off being straightedge. I like a lot of the straightedge punk as well, Fugazi and Ian MacKaye especially, what he has done with The Evens and Coriky.

Slaughterhouse Prayer *deals unflinchingly with an unpopular subject, confronting the debate over the horror meted out to domestic animals from a moral high ground. Koushik Banerjea speaks of your "fundamental decency" and this profoundly basic ethic stands behind all of your writing. Isn't fundamental decency a myth of the British working class?*

I like to think most people are fundamentally decent. I appreciate that's odd given the cruelties we inflict, and there are plenty of times when I feel the opposite way. Human beings can convince themselves of anything, can't they? We are constantly justifying our behaviour, and *Slaughterhouse Prayer* looks at this in some depth. The novel is as much about the human condition and the wider society as it is about what we are doing to non-human animals. It is all connected. Can't be separated off.

I suppose the ability to self-deceive is a survival tool. Fitting in, inventing and accepting new truths, losing ourselves in the mass, strength in numbers. We are rooted in mimicry – language, behaviour, appearance, culture, thought. It is far easier to agree with those around us than disagree. The same applies to those who blindly accept the system and those who blindly oppose the system. Basic stuff, I know. Yet when it comes to our abuse of animals I am sure that deep down most people know what they are doing is wrong. This is why jokes are made, the sort of belittling 'humour' that isn't applied to the chopping of a carrot, for instance. Animals have to be mocked and belittled – *stupid, dirty, smelly.*

I wouldn't say it is a myth of the British working class in particular, and I wouldn't say it is necessarily a myth, either. In Britain's case there is a fundamental decency embedded in the post-war welfare state. I have just finished re-reading *The Grapes Of Wrath* after many years, and I was blown away all over again. That decency is core to the novel. People sticking together against the odds. Doing their best to help each other out.

It is true that through my novels I have tried to even certain things out, show those so often stereotyped and dismissed in a more honest light. I want to show the positives rather than the endless negatives. I have felt this since I was young, that the official portrayal – whether through politicians, the ruling classes, their lackeys, the media, the controllers of the so-called arts – too often bears little resemblance to reality.

Here, the National Health Service is the last of our great nationalised industries, and it is still revered, a public institution rooted in that decency you mention, the belief that something as essential as our health shouldn't be monetised. My novel *White Trash* based around an NHS nurse, emphasises the worth of every single individual, insists that their stories and feelings count, that they aren't 'white trash'. The villain of the piece is very similar to the worst character to be found in *Slaughterhouse Prayer*.

What sort of music did you grow up listening to? Did you have a relatively straightforward evolution of taste, with pop songs on the radio giving way to rock vinyl, then punk and then Oi! and on to other sounds, or were you into other types of music from an early age?

I was lucky in that my father played the piano – boogie-woogie / barrelhouse blues – so I was hearing that at home since I was small, along with his blues and Rolling Stones records. Jerry Lee Lewis and Kitty Wells. My first gig was aged around six months when my parents went to visit the great Pete Johnson and I sat on his knee as he played the piano. They may have gone twice, although I was sadly too young to remember. I wish cameras had been used more in those days. Pete Johnson was one of the Big Four of boogie-woogie along with Albert Ammons, Meade Lux Lewis and Jimmy Yancey. Dad met Meade Lux Lewis as well, and he played with Memphis Slim and Sonny Boy Williamson in London.

He recorded a couple of solo albums on small labels, and in the Sixties was in a band called Dharma Blues, which put out an album and a single. They are the first group I saw live, the first gig I can recall. They were rehearsing in the ground floor flat where we lived at the time, so I was probably seven or eight years old. I clearly remember them playing the Lead Belly song 'Where Did You Sleep Last Night'. It is a crystal-clear memory. Around that time we saw Dave Brock busking on Portobello Road in Notting Hill. Dave was in the first version of Dharma Blues before he left to form Hawkwind.

It was an interest for my dad, and he never made money out of his music, but he was very well regarded, knew the likes of Eric Clapton and Charlie Watts back before they became famous. He played by ear, performed at some legendary London venues – the 100 Club and Marquee in London among them – and was a regular at Eel Pie Island. In the Seventies he would play two or three nights a week in the pubs around Brentford.

Otherwise it was the usual route for me – as a boy there were all those Sixties songs on the radio, buying an early Beatles EP and falling in love with Sandie Shaw; then around eleven or twelve I got into David Bowie, plus the glam rock of the first half of the Seventies, especially Slade and Sweet; and when I was that age when we find 'our music', fifteen or sixteen, punk arrived. Hearing Doctor Feelgood's *Malpractice* album was a big moment, more so 'Sheena Is A Punk Rocker' by the Ramones at a Friday night disco in Slough, and things kept getting better and better with the Sex Pistols singles and the first Clash album. That LP took things to another level for me.

There was so much music around at the time. Reggae and dub were parallels to punk, while there was rock n roll and Teddy Boy pubs, a big soul scene, disco and jazz funk, heavy rock and greasers. I have always liked Led Zeppelin. *Physical Graffiti* – what a brilliant album. Punk was quick to change, X-Ray Spex and Sham 69 following the Clash and the Pistols and moving into the Ruts and the Lurkers, both of which were local bands for me, and in time there were the Last Resort, the Business and so on, as well as the psychobilly / rockabilly boom. In many ways Oi was the real punk. The fans were in the bands now, and they stripped the music back, kicked out the hippie influence.

I feel I have broad tastes, but can't get into disco and that sort of stuff, struggle with jazz although I keep trying. At heart, I am a punk, love how it has evolved. I like the better drum 'n' bass, techno, hip hop, especially trip hop – Tricky and DJ Shadow. It is amazing how their records are constructed. I saw

DJ Shadow at the Forum in Kentish Town a couple of times, and the first of those shows was one of the best I have ever experienced.

Did you listen mostly for the lyrics or the tunes? Ever try learning to play an instrument? Sing? Write songs?
At first it would have been the tunes, simple songs with melody, but as I say, Bowie was and remains special – I love his *Ziggy Stardust / Diamond Dogs* period, and then how he went to Berlin and reinvented himself with *Low* and *Lodger*. While his words were interesting in their way, they were more like collages, while punk was direct and said something about our lives. I remember Johnny Rotten saying his lyrics were his literature, and that seemed so right to me. It still does.

It was that first Clash album that made me want to write, or at least planted a seed, a vague idea, as I would never have thought myself capable. There wasn't a love song to be heard on *The Clash*. The lyrics were about the world I knew, the things I was thinking about. It was pretty incredible really, discovering that sort of storytelling, and I wondered why there weren't novels like this, serious books rather than the teenage pulp that was around. Again, this is a clear memory.

I worked the reasons out in time, learned that publishing is in the hands of a certain class, that for the most part those in control release stories that reflect their lives rather than ours. That and a snobbery which says the proles don't or can't read books. There are honourable exceptions, individuals and publishers that truly believe in literature, its importance and how it should belong to everyone, and there are periods when a different sort of writer breaks through, but they are eased into the background in time, ignored or treated as a gimmick.

I can't play an instrument, but I have written some songs with Leigh Heggarty from Ruts DC. Well, we have written an album based on *The Prison House*, but it stalled and has been at the demo stage for years. At the moment I am putting together some songs with Andy Town out of Knock Off. In both cases I write the lyrics, give some input with regards the sound. I wish I was more musical. Rather than playing an instrument, I would love to know how to operate a recording studio.

How did the Human Punk shows at the 100 Club come about? What's your role in making them happen? Most memorable gigs there?

I had spoken to a couple of friends about doing something in Central London focusing on bands from London and the surrounding areas. Andy Chesham and Mark Wyeth had put on nights before, and been collaborating at Club Ska where some of the ska and bluebeat greats played. I was a regular at Club Ska, and they had read my novel *Human Punk*, suggested we do it under that name as a reflection of the book. Mark moved away not long after, so I have been doing it with Andy for the majority of the time since we started in 2014. There have been many memorable nights, but early on we did Sham 69 and the place was heaving. Short, sharp, shocks to the system. Truly brilliant. But there have been many special gigs over the years.

We have tried to match established bands who are still producing with younger, newer groups, and three of those we have promoted since we started are Knock Off, Crown Court and Tear Up. They are three of my favourite bands, and those are always memorable shows. And I have learned to DJ, really enjoy doing it as well, thanks to Andy. He is Doctor Vinyl and I am JK Herbert. Human Punk On 45. We only play vinyl and it has made me dig out my old singles, think about the music in new ways. I can play some decent sets now – punk, glam, rockabilly, Oi. I enjoy it, anyway.

Harlan Ellison after being asked, "Where do you get your ideas" one too many times, replied, "Schenectady." Where do you get your ideas?
Nertwold World… No, my ideas come out of my life, the things I know and the things I think about, my feelings and beliefs, all those dreams and fears and hopes that fill our heads. I draw on my experiences. More so in some books than others. Not for the actual stories, but the settings and reference points. I am never short of ideas. It is more a case of keeping them under control. Staying focused.

Are you one of those writers who's constantly jotting down things in a notebook, and if so, do your stories grow out of that process? Do you outline the entire novel (the "road map" approach) or do you wing it and see where it takes you?
I don't jot things down, no, although maybe I should do, but I tend to remember the better ideas. I will make a note in a file on my laptop sometimes, but I am always thinking about my writing so they keep swirling around. I do have files set up with titles, have always felt that the right name for a book is essential, that the whole thing is there waiting to be written

if that's in place. Does that make sense? It varies with each book how far I go in planning it out. Some I have sat down and set off with nothing but the title, others I have a rough structure worked out. Some of these are rougher than others. But I prefer to keep things loose, build and tighten as I go. It is less restrictive, leaves me with more options. That is the fun of writing. The challenge. It is much more exciting this way. There is always a goal, though, knowing what the book is about in a broader sense.

Are you self-taught or did you take any writing classes? Is it getting any easier/harder to write after ten novels? How many drafts do you typically go through?

Self-taught. I have never taken a writing class, didn't go to university, found my own way through trial and error. And a lot of work. I am diligent in what I do, believe I am a decent editor. I am certainly not lazy. The editing process is as much fun for me as the actual writing, taking those first attempts and moving them on and adding layers. I love how new ideas emerge, how characters and situations can lead me rather than the other way round. I am strict with myself, but don't always write in a straight line, more like loops, which is one of the joys of using a laptop.

It is easier to write after ten novels. Every time I finish a book, another one or two suggest themselves. There are always ideas I would like to expand, take in other directions. The thing that gets in the way is everyday life. That is what slows me down.

Let's talk about the film adaptation of your first novel, The Football Factory. *How did that come about?*
The book came out in 1996 and I was lucky that it sold word-of-mouth – around 60,000 copies with Jonathan Cape in the first year, and a lot more when it went into the Vintage paperback. It had sold over 200,000 copies before the film was made, so it was one of those books that were well-known before the adaptation. The film was made on a small budget, and the extras were all people who went to football. It was authentic and had a dynamic. I had got to know the director Nick Love in the late Nineties, and for a while he was developing my novel *Headhunters,* so things evolved from there. The film of *The Football Factory* came out in 2004.

Were you involved in writing the screenplay? Or at least consulted?
I was consulted, yes. Nick and I discussed the screenplay he wrote, both before he started and once he had produced the first and second drafts. I stayed in the mix for a long time, but there comes a point when you move into the background.

Were you ever on the set? A "Hitchcock-type" cameo anywhere in the film?
If you look carefully in the pub scene before the Millwall Away part you might see me. Don't blink, though.

After more than twenty years, what did you honestly think of the film version?
Once you get involved in film, see the complexities involved, the influences that come with investment, the number of

people trying to have their say, you realise what can go wrong. I'm not one of those writers who could just sign away their work without another thought, especially in the case of *The Football Factory*, given the subject matter. But Nick knows that world and he did a great job. The film doesn't have the same depth or clear politics as the novel, but that is the case with most adaptations. They are different mediums. Film is more about showing than telling. The source material had to be streamlined to make it work. The film has great energy and humour. It has a soul. I am proud of what Nick achieved. It was important for both of us that it was done right.

In 1976 punk changed the cultural landscape: Many of us cisgender males have been on the front lines of the class struggle since 1976. Yet today, defiant, working-class men are still challenged, even cancelled, by being disparagingly lumped in with the "patriarchy." You've addressed this injustice in your work and in other interviews. Isn't this essentially sexist bias on the part of all self-righteous non-males who share this approach, playing right into the hands of the opposition?

I believe so. If someone's view is dismissed solely on the grounds that they are white, working-class and middle-aged – that is racist, classist, ageist. As well as being pretty stupid. I think social media and the way it has shut down discussion means those with the power to lose people their jobs and have them ostracised are too scared to challenge the bullies for fear of being bullied themselves. It shows their isolation, how they are stuck in bubbles reacting to keyboard warriors with too much time on their hands. It works all ways, doesn't matter the position of those trying to shut down debate.

It is worrying to think where all this is heading, but it suits those behind the scenes to break us up into smaller and smaller groups, set us against each other. These are backwards steps. Otherwise prosperous, healthy, privileged individuals decide they are suffering terribly due to a comment online. This shifts the focus from what really matters, questions of wealth distribution and class. Which is, I suppose, the point.

You've said elsewhere that growing up, you (unlike most writers) weren't a big reader. When did that change, and is your work, in general, less influenced by all that has been written before, by not having all the usual fictions internalized at an early age?
Maybe I was being unfair on myself, as I read more than my friends, but I wasn't studying the classics when I was eleven years old, couldn't get excited about stuffy novels set in country houses full of upper-class twits. I found the prose as dull as the subject matter. I was more into music, but started reading more seriously in my later teens I would say, although it is hard to put dates on that now. I found American writers far more interesting than those from England. There wasn't the same class bias, and their writing style was more fluid, had a greater energy, the characters easier to relate to and admire, even from a distance. There was a great sense of freedom about many of those American novels.

The English authors I liked early on were George Orwell and Alan Sillitoe, Aldous Huxley's *Brave New World*, and then came European writers such as Zola, Camus and Kafka – *The*

Earth, The Outsider, Metamorphosis. Alan Sillitoe's *Saturday Night And Sunday Morning* and *The Loneliness Of The Long-Distance Runner* struck a chord even though written twenty years earlier and set in the Midlands. I got to know Alan after I was published. Myself and Martin Knight became good friends with him, which was pretty amazing. He was our mate. But going back, I got into Jack Kerouac and he made an impression on me with *On The Road* and *Dharma Bums* in particular. Those books made me want to travel, which I did later with one- and two-month trips into Europe, and then from my mid-twenties a couple of year-long journeys into the wider world.

I wrote two books before *The Football Factory.* One in my early twenties when I was working in a warehouse that was closing down and I was thinking about George Orwell. *Running Through Glass* touches on *White Trash* in many ways, but I forgot about the manuscript for years, even thought about throwing it out when it turned up, glad now that I didn't. I have been wondering whether to update it one day, as it is future-set and could work as part of a trilogy coming out of *The Liberal Politics Of Adolf Hitler.*

After the first of my longer travels I wrote this huge manuscript that is nearly two hundred thousand words long! It is very naive. Perhaps I wanted to be Jack Kerouac by this point. I spent five months in India and stayed in an ashram for a while, and in Thailand I was in a Buddhist monastery for two months, did a couple of ten-day meditation retreats while there. Halfway through the second retreat my head went into orbit and stayed there for several months. As well as Thailand I went to Sri Lanka, Nepal and Burma. So I wrote this huge manuscript on the back of that trip when I got back to England – spaced out. Again, I should do something with it one day, reshape it when I am old and looking back – maybe call it *The Boy Who Searched For God*. It would be a lot of work.

I read Burroughs, but while his methods were interesting, and he was referenced by Bowie, I found his books boring, and he was a suspect character, to put it mildly. DJ Shadow is far better, even without the words. Same sort of idea, to my mind. After Kerouac I was reading Hubert Selby Jr, Charles Bukowski, Hunter S Thompson, Nelson Algren, Upton Sinclair, John Steinbeck, Jack London, later moving to the Fantes John and Dan, Thom Jones, John O'Brien and so on. And the original *On The Road* – Woody Guthrie's *Bound For Glory*.

I doubt that brave, working-class, free-flowing American literature exists today. But going back to your question, I wasn't formally trained and I do feel that has been helpful, that it has given me a lot more freedom.

What did you read before this?

I read CS Lewis as a child, and then Enid Blyton, from fantasy to solving mysteries. Kids left alone to do what they want in big houses, allowed to roam as they please. Those sort of books continually repeat. When I was a bit older I read a lot of Agatha Christie, her more serious mysteries dealing in murder. I am sure some of that early reading left its mark.

It was interesting when Kevin Williamson told me he was an Agatha Christie fan – Kevin published *Rebel Inc* magazine, where I first made it into print. When I was twelve or thirteen, like a million boys in England, I read the Richard Allen skinhead books and Mick Norman Hell's Angels series. These were exploitative pulp, but lapped up by youngsters who wanted to read about subjects that interested them. This is one of the reasons that Clash album made me think there should be a different sort of literature.

You've mentioned that an upcoming novel will be set in America. I know it's still early in the process, but how do you envision this differing from your British novels?
My mum was American and a great storyteller. She grew up in San Francisco, and the city she knew before coming to England was very different to the city portrayed since the beatniks arrived. She left me with lots of family stories and impressions of the Sunset District where she grew up. Along with my love of American literature, that is another motivation. I don't know how much the actual style would differ, although I would clearly have to think about some of the language, especially the spoken word and any use of slang. It would be an exciting thing to do. Emotional, too. I have thought about it for a long time. It would need to be written on location.

You've said very briefly, in passing, somewhere, that you spent time in prison. Care to elaborate? How did that impact writing The Prison House*?*
I served two months of a ten-month sentence in a Greek prison at the tender age of twenty-two for getting into a fight while drunk. It was an excessive sentence, as along with a friend we

were basically defending ourselves, but we weren't blameless and as foreigners the court cracked down hard. The prison was a rough place. A shock to the system. But I survived and used it as the setting for *The Prison House*. The story is fictional, but the conditions and atmosphere are based on reality. There are certain subjects I don't think those who haven't experienced them should attempt, and being locked up in prison is one of these.

As a famous author, how are you preparing for your "legacy"? Have an institution in mind (or is one already in place) for storing (and making available for study) your papers, early drafts, correspondence etc.?
Would anyone be interested!? I have an old chest of drawers in my office and have put various papers in there over the years. I find things when having a tidy-up – folders of old stories, those manuscripts I mentioned, all sorts of stuff. It is strange rediscovering so many words. I haven't thought about this, to be honest.

While not as reclusive as, say, a JD Salinger or a Thomas Pynchon (you do book signings and regularly attend the Rebellion Festival in Blackpool, etc.) for such a popular, contemporary author very little is known about your personal history. Care to fill in some blanks for those of us who have followed your writing and have wondered about the guy behind these fascinating novels?
When I was first published I avoided publicity as much as I could, and didn't want to do live events. It was down to a mixture of shyness and the feeling that I wouldn't be much good.

I would never read from one of my novels and couldn't give a straight talk, but now I am fine when interviewed. I never minded the radio, just never listen to myself afterwards. Given the nature of those early novels I didn't fancy going down the predictable routes. I wanted to focus on my writing.

I do feel that an author is better off letting their books speak for them, although now I am older and have a varied body of work behind me it can be nice to discuss things. It reminds me why I wrote these novels, and that in turn makes me want to write more. I first started doing events when I went to France for my translations as I felt safe going through the filter of an interpreter, and I was chuffed at how well I was treated there, the respect I was shown. The French take literature seriously. That gave me the confidence to do one or two things here in England. I find it easy these days.

What other jobs have you had?

I worked at various jobs before becoming an author – stacking shelves in a supermarket while at school; unloading and loading lorries in a warehouse after I left; driving a forklift in a factory; painting houses; packing roses in a flower market; working on a van; labouring; in a local council office dealing with housing claims; sub-editing on a magazine; some travel articles after I went travelling. I even worked as a doorman once. But only the once.

Did you always want to write?

Like a lot of boys I wanted to be a footballer, and as a teenager I wanted to be in a band. I didn't do anything about this, of course. Apparently, when I was small I planned to join the Japanese army when I grew up. It must have been reading the *Commando* comics that gave me the idea.

Where did your decision to start writing science fiction come from?
I was thinking to write about the internet and where it is taking us, and I wanted to write about the European Union and where that is going, but as two separate books, and then it struck me to combine them and set the novel in the future. I don't know why I never tried this before. It is odd as *Nineteen Eighty-Four*, *Brave New World* and *Fahrenheit 451* were big books for me, and as a child I loved the Supermarionation series on television – *Captain Scarlet* and *Joe 90* but especially *Thunderbirds* – and later *Star Trek*, those old sci-fi B-movies. There was HG Wells as well, and when I was older Philip K Dick. The film *Blade Runner* based on *Do Androids Dream Of Electric Sheep?* is one of my favourite movies.

I wrote *The Liberal Politics Of Adolf Hitler*, and while it isn't exactly 'science fiction' it is I suppose 'dystopian'. 'Machine Elves Descending' is closer to straight science fiction, further out there, even if like most SF it is about today. It has been nice, playing with the language as much as anything, being able to shuffle and invent words. I have always said what I want in my novels, drift into imaginary worlds, because that is what humans beings do, but this has given me new possibilities. I hope to write more along these lines. There is so much scope there and I am halfway through a long short at the moment – "Klub Foot Affair". And have started a spin-off "Call Me Elvis". There is always a spin-off… *The Liberal*

Politics was the easiest book I have ever written. The most fun. I have started writing a sequel.

And the hardest?
Slaughterhouse Prayer. I struggled given the subject matter and the things that were going on in my life at the time. I rewrote it twice. Went back to the beginning and started again. I was on a mission. I felt that getting the book right would be the culmination of everything I had tried to do – *The Football Factory Trilogy* and the idea that politics has been hijacked and the masses are left fighting among themselves; *Human Punk* and *Skinheads* focusing on music, 'subcultures' and the individuals within those; *White Trash* as a defence of the NHS and the common people; *The Prison House* with its characters out on the margins of society; and then *Slaughterhouse Prayer* which goes beyond those margins. I felt that if I got the book right I could die knowing I had got to where I had been heading since the start. I feel I achieved that in terms of the subject matter and the style. Mind you, a week later that post-publication emptiness opened up and I needed to write again.

They are very different in their style and tone.
I like to vary things, even though there is a thread running through all my work. Another positive of the Clash was how they experimented. They weren't afraid to change. Some songs worked, other didn't. *Sandinista!* is such a great album. Six sides of vinyl. They took in lots of the music I like – punk, reggae, dub, rockabilly. It was the same with David Bowie. He wasn't going to be bossed around by the suits. Paul Weller did

likewise when he broke up The Jam. I wish he hadn't, but I respect the fact that he wanted to follow his own path. Maybe it is a little harder with novels, but I believe we should at least try. It makes things much more interesting.

It's apparent in your work that you have a spiritual side, but not in a traditional, organized religion sense. How were you raised, and how did you arrive at your current beliefs?

Myself and my two sisters weren't raised with religion. It was the same with my friends growing up. My mum was Catholic and my dad Protestant, but they rarely went to church. My mum drew on her religion more towards the end of her life, and she had lived with the nuns for a while when she was two or three years old, yet she was the most open-minded person you could meet. My dad had different sides to him. He was a pub man with lots of friends, a maverick who loved playing the piano, and he was interested in different strands of thought – meditation, UFOs, crop circles. His family were Spiritualists.

My grandmother practised psychometry and my Auntie Lucy was a medium. A lot of people in Britain became interested in Spiritualism after the losses of the First World War, the sheer trauma of its aftermath. I have been to the Spiritualist Church at different times in my life. I wouldn't say I have solid beliefs, but I do think anything is possible. When I travelled in the East I looked into things more, and following my parents' deaths I realised that I believe in an afterlife. I do think each of us has a soul, and that there is a mass consciousness under the surface along with our subconscious, that at some deep level we maybe know everything that has happened and everything that is going to happen.

I am scared of death so it might be wishful thinking, but so what? I don't care if I am making it up or not, trying to convince myself. Humans live fantasy existences, anyway, create our own fictions. I think that fear of death is there in all my novels. The wasting of precious time. I don't feel I am unusual. How can anyone not care about dying? Religion developed to offer us answers, some sort of structure and meaning, but it became corrupted. It is as if in our modern society those basic questions are no longer being asked. I'm not saying we should go back to those controlling times again, not saying that at all, but there is a fear that makes us behave in terrible ways. If we didn't fear death, knew or truly believed we lived forever, would there be any more greed or any more wars?

Verbal 11 *has a lengthy interview with Iain Sinclair, and he's written an introduction for London Books' edition of Robert Westerby's* Wide Boys Never Work. *How does his work resonate with your interests?*
I like the way Iain writes, that staccato style he has perfected, and much of his work links to my love of London and its history. Peter Ackroyd and Michael Moorcock's London writing is special, and when I discovered those Thirties authors, people such as James Curtis, Gerald Kersh and Simon Blumenfeld, it was like cutting through time. The style and vibrancy of their writing is incredible – the reason for the London Classics list I edit and publish through London Books, which I own with Martin Knight.

A loaded question: Do intelligent, informed, aware people have a moral and ethical responsibility (by writing novels, for instance) to help those less gifted? Or should they just use their smarts for getting rich?

Define intelligent, informed, aware… Everyone has their own gifts. I honestly believe that to be true. And no, I don't think trying to get rich is a good use of our limited time.

Bibliography

NOVELS

The Football Factory (1996)
Headhunters (1997)
England Away (1998)
Human Punk (2000)
White Trash (2001)
The Prison House (2004)
Skinheads (2008)
The Liberal Politics Of Adolf Hitler (2016)
Slaughterhouse Prayer (2018)
London Country (2023)

NOVELLAS

The Beasts Of Brussels (2020)
Grand Union (2023)
Peekaboo Bosh (2025)

ANTHOLOGIES

John King Omnibus (2000)
Machine Elves Descending (2026)

About The Author

John King is the author of ten novels and three novellas to date. His first, *The Football Factory*, was an immediate word-of-mouth success and was subsequently turned into a high-profile film. His stories reflect his interests – particularly music, subcultures, pubs and travel – while challenging a range of stereotypes that are often accepted by the established political factions. Common themes are powerlessness and enemy-creation, the contradictions found in every walk of life. Before becoming an author King worked at a variety of jobs and spent two years travelling around the world in the late 1980s. He has long been associated with fanzines and the small-press world, running *Two Sevens* in the early 1990s, while also writing for more mainstream titles such as the *New Statesman*, *Le Monde* and *la Repubblica*. He currently publishes and edits *Verbal*, a fiction-based publication. King co-owns the independent publisher London Books and co-runs Human Punk nights in Central London, where he DJs between bands. He lives in London.

FRIENDS OF PM

These are indisputably momentous times—the financial system is melting down globally and the Empire is stumbling. Now more than ever there is a vital need for radical ideas.

In the years since its founding—and on a mere shoestring—PM Press has risen to the formidable challenge of publishing and distributing knowledge and entertainment for the struggles ahead. With hundreds of releases to date, we have published an impressive and stimulating array of literature, art, music, politics, and culture. Using every available medium, we've succeeded in connecting those hungry for ideas and information to those putting them into practice.

Friends of PM allows you to directly help impact, amplify, and revitalize the discourse and actions of radical writers, filmmakers, and artists. It provides us with a stable foundation from which we can build upon our early successes and provides a much-needed subsidy for the materials that can't necessarily pay their own way. You can help make that happen—and receive every new title automatically delivered to your door once a month—by joining as a Friend of PM Press. And, we'll throw in a free T-shirt when you sign up.

Here are your options:

- $30 a month: Get all books and pamphlets plus 50% discount on all webstore purchases
- $40 a month: Get all PM Press releases (including CDs and DVDs) plus 50% discount on all webstore purchases
- $100 a month: Superstar—Everything plus PM merchandise, free downloads, and 50% discount on all webstore purchases

For those who can't afford $30 or more a month, we have Sustainer Rates at $15, $10, and $5. Sustainers get a free PM Press T-shirt and a 50% discount on all purchases from our website.

Your Visa or Mastercard will be billed once a month, until you tell us to stop. Or until our efforts succeed in bringing the revolution around. Or the financial meltdown of Capital makes plastic redundant. Whichever comes first.

PM Press is an independent, radical publisher of critically necessary books for our tumultuous times. Our aim is to deliver bold political ideas and vital stories to all walks of life and arm the dreamers to demand the impossible. Founded in 2007 by a small group of people with decades of publishing, media, and organizing experience, we have sold millions of copies of our books, most often one at a time, face to face. We're old enough to know what we're doing and young enough to know what's at stake. Join us to create a better world.

PM Press
PO Box 23912
Oakland, CA 94623
info@pmpress.org

PM Press in Europe
europe@pmpress.org
www.pmpress.org.uk